THE ~~PERFECT~~ DATE

IRIS BAXTER

© 2023 by Iris Baxter

All rights reserved. No portion of this book may be reproduced mechanically, electronically, or by any other means, including photocopying, without permission of the publisher or author except in the case of brief quotations embodied in critical articles and reviews. It is illegal to copy this book, post it to a website, or distribute it by any other means without permission from the publisher or author.

Contents

Part 1 5

Chapter 1 7

Chapter 2 11

Chapter 3 17

Chapter 4 27

Chapter 5 31

Chapter 6 37

Chapter 7 41

Chapter 8 49

Chapter 9 57

Chapter 10 69

Chapter 11 73

Chapter 12 79

Part 2 87

Chapter 13 89

Chapter 14 93

Chapter 15 101

Chapter 16 107

Chapter 17 113

Chapter 18 119

Chapter 19 123

Chapter 20 133

Chapter 21 139

Epilogue 149

Part 1

Chapter 1

How did I get myself into this situation?

That's what I keep asking myself as I rub my numb hands and wipe the tears off my face. My chest is tight, unable to let proper amounts of air in, and my legs feel like they're about to buckle under my weight.

In hindsight, it's my own fault, but I want to say that I can't put all the blame on myself.

After months of finding duds on Tinder (Seriously, that app needs to have a psychological evaluation upon registration), dozens of disastrous dates that had me questioning my standards, and countless times being ghosted, I was too desperate to believe that my date tonight was a lucky break for me.

Sean looked handsome in his profile pic. Having been burned before by meeting guys who looked nothing like the pictures that so cleverly hid their blemishes, I knew to curb my expectations when we agreed to go out on this date.

Hey, I promise I'm not shallow, nor am I judgmental of people who try to look their best in pictures.

We all do that, don't we? We hold our breaths with our tummies tucked in, or we conveniently place the camera in a way that our rolls of fat aren't in the frame, or we find a spot with good lighting that hides those pesky flaws on our cheeks and foreheads.

I know I do.

Everyone wants to feel attractive but some of us more so. If you've ever been in a relationship where nothing you ever did was good enough for your partner, you know what I'm talking about. By the time you're single again, a cute Starbucks employee could draw a heart next to your name, or someone at the gym could tell you they're noticing a difference in your looks, and you'd be hung up on the comments for the entire day.

Compliments are addictive. No wonder so many people resort to catfishing. I once texted with a guy who sent me a selfie of himself, only he forgot to remove the search caption above that said "average guy selfie." Gotta give him credit, though.

At least, he didn't post a picture of a ridiculously handsome model and claim it was him.

The reason why I'm saying all of this is because, when I decided to go out on a date with Sean earlier tonight, I had no expectations about his appearance. We had texted a little bit, and I liked the vibe I had gotten from him.

Sean in person was a lot different than the pictures he had sent me. When I say different, I mean different *better*. In fact, his Tinder pics could do no justice to the person standing in front of the *Picnic Place* restaurant.

I remember mouthing "wow" to myself and hoping he wouldn't notice the awe on my face. I suddenly felt inadequate compared to him, but I didn't want him to get the idea that he had the upper hand.

Maybe it wasn't Sean's physical appearance itself but the aura of confidence he emitted.

"Hi. I'm Melissa," I said.

I detected a nice musk, which I instantly recognized as Tom Ford.

When Sean put his hand forward for a shake and smiled, I knew I had struck gold by matching with this man.

An hour later, I'm locked in the basement of his apartment and begging him to let me out.

Chapter 2

It's hard for me to focus on what Sean is saying as I stare at his eyes.

One thing that made me swipe right as soon as I saw his picture was the ocean-blue eyes. Staring at them under the dim restaurant lights and watching them morph from blue to gray to a shade of green is mesmerizing.

"What about you?" he asks.

"What?" I ask, completely oblivious to what he had said just prior to that question.

He smiles in a way that tells me he's not upset that I'm not paying attention. In fact, is it just my imagination, or does that smile tell me he finds me cute? I find myself hoping that's the case.

Focus, Melissa. He's expecting an answer. What was he talking about just before?

When we first arrived, he asked me if the place was to my liking and, if not, whether I wanted to go someplace else. I had asked him what he does for a living, and he told me he works for a marketing agency. I asked him to tell me about the job, and he went on to explain what it is that he does. It wasn't a boring explanation or anything like that, it's just... those eyes.

"What I asked was: What's your job like? You said you work as a teaching assistant, right?" he asks.

"Oh, right," I say and quickly hide behind my glass of red wine.

Yet another pang of inadequacy hits me as I ponder the fact that he works in a big, corporate company while I talk to children in simplified English.

Oh, sure. My job is as exciting as yours. Sure, I don't have meetings with clients from other big companies daily, and I don't broker million-dollar deals, but I get to prepare the classroom for the real teacher—the one who gets paid double my salary—listen to children read things aloud, and help grade homework and tests.

Don't get me wrong, I love my job, but it's nowhere as exciting and dynamic as what Sean described for his work. It's my turn to speak, but I feel like I'm about to give a mediocre presentation after the student who just aced it and set the expectations for the entire classroom.

"It's a lot more docile than your job," I say.

"A lot less stressful, too, I assume," Sean says.

"Not sure. Have you ever been forced to spend six hours in a room with screaming kids asking questions you already answered ten times?"

"Sounds like my daily meetings with the other departments."

I laugh at that. Not only is Sean handsome, successful, and smart, but he also has a great sense of humor. It's really difficult to find somebody who appreciates humor. My humor anyway.

I cannot tell you how many times I got blocked or left on read on Tinder because of a joke or pickup line I made. When I first joined the app, I took things very seriously. A few dates were enough to help me figure out that being myself from the get-go was like a filter for all the guys it wouldn't work out with. The moment I let loose was the moment the quality of my dates started improving... somewhat.

A ringing sound punctuates the jazz music in the background. Sean straightens his back, and a look of disappointment crosses his face. He reaches into his pocket and pulls his phone out. After staring at it for a moment, he touches the screen, and the ringing stops.

"Sorry about that." He looks at me. "I forgot to mute this damn thing."

"I don't mind," I say. "A busy working man like you... I'd imagine your phone ringing all day long."

He laughs. "It was just my friend checking up on me."

"If you want to call him back..."

"No, no. It's all good. He calls me way too often anyway. I can't just drop everything whenever he rings me up."

Some silence lingers between us. I can't not notice the fact that all the guests in the restaurant are speaking in hushed tones, as if not to disturb the silence. It sort of feels like we're in a library. I don't mind. There's nothing more obnoxious than going out to eat or watch a movie, knowing there's always that one family that doesn't care how loud and obtrusive they are.

"So, you must be really good if you got to your position so fast," I say.

Sean shakes his head. "I just do my best and work hard. I'm not any more talented or smarter than the next employee."

He's humble. I like that even if it's fake humble. So far, Sean has given me no reason to believe he thinks he's more superior just because he has a successful career.

"But honestly, I don't think I'll stay here long," he says.

"Why's that?"

"The money's good, but I don't see myself doing this forever. It's too many hours and often infringes on my personal life. If I ever get married and have kids, I want to be able to devote my time to my family, and not the company. And right now, I try to find time for my own hobbies, like going to the gym, jogging, and acting classes twice a week."

Suddenly, I find myself liking Sean even more. Not only is he successful, but he's dedicated to his hobbies, and he's a man who has his priorities straight, at least in the lane of what I consider to be right. Moreover, in the past thirty minutes that we've been speaking, Sean says something on more than one occasion that's to my liking. On top of that, he's a gentleman, and he's been nothing but respectful to me.

Earlier tonight, when I got dressed, put on my makeup, and left my apartment to meet Sean, I did so without any expectations. I'm a person who doesn't think about what will happen next until it happens.

Half an hour with Sean, and I'm already picturing us watching movies together snuggled up against each other, having pillow talks, talking about meeting each other's parents, and so on.

Please tell me we all fantasize like that about the people we like.

I wonder if Sean's only saying things he thinks I want to hear. No, that's unlikely. He doesn't know me that well. Aiming to say something I like—and guess it—would be a hell of a lucky shot in the dark.

Besides, Sean seems genuine. He's a nice guy who clearly just wants to find someone he can hold hands and cuddle with. Maybe he's been through the same stuff as I. The same toxic relationship that toppled his self-esteem to the ground as mine did to me. Maybe he was just looking for a new start, away from the familiar.

I can't help but compare Sean to Joshua. The two are like water and fire. Sean is everything I secretly wished throughout my entire relationship Joshua would have been. I want to tell Sean how happy I am to hear that we're compatible on that level, but I stop myself again before I can do that.

I may be desperate, but that doesn't mean I have to show it, especially not on our first date.

Just then, my phone buzzes in my pocket. I ask Sean to give me a second and explain that my roommate Rachel is probably worried about me. The message I've received is not from Rachel, though.

Please, just answer me. I swear I can make this right.

The number is not in my contacts anymore, but I recognize it. I would recognize it any time of the day or night.

It's Joshua.

"Everything okay?" Sean asks.

He must have noticed the look of dread on my face. I smile, quickly block the number—which I should have done so long ago—tuck the phone into my pocket, and nod. It takes me another long moment to compose myself.

A number of questions run in my head: What does Joshua want? Does he know I'm on a date and wants to stop me from hooking up with Sean? Is he watching me right now?

I feel the urge to look around, but I suppress it. I am not going to let him ruin my date with Sean.

"I feel the same way. About personal life and marriage, I mean," I say, taking a sip of my wine.

I almost say that my ex and I didn't see eye to eye in that regard, but I gulp, deciding it would be rude to talk about Joshua on my first date with Sean.

Please don't scare this man away, Melissa.

I keep referring to it as a "first date" as if I've already decided in my mind that another one would happen. As far as I'm concerned, it will. Sean would need to show me a really dark secret to convince me to run away.

Boy, was I blind to the red flags.

Chapter 3

We order food after the waiter finally notices us. Sean apologizes for the waiter's delay as if it's his fault. I don't mind. I'm completely enthralled by my conversation with him and have forgotten about the food—and Joshua's desperate text.

He orders a steak right after he makes sure I'm not vegan or vegetarian. I have a carbonara. The food arrives fairly fast, and I can see why Sean has chosen this place. The presentation on the plates is superb. I have a bite to make sure the taste is on par. It is.

"I've lived in this city for over ten years, and I didn't know about this place," I say.

"Yeah, they need to amp up their advertising," Sean says as he stabs the steak with the fork.

Juices flow from the meat as he slices into it.

"Maybe you can help them," I quip.

"I don't usually work with these kinds of clients." He smiles. "I mean, I work with companies promoting food, but it's usually someone who paid thousands of dollars to have his cereal shown on social media."

"Do you have any favorite clients?"

"There's a footwear company that's so grateful that I helped them improve their business that they send me limited edition tennis shoes every month. I have an entire closet full of those."

"Wow."

It's obvious Sean takes great pride in his career. I'm glad for him. Yes, I know he wants to change positions in the future, but I'm also glad he loves what he's doing.

"Enough about work." He waves a hand. "I talk about it twenty-four-seven."

"With work taking up so much of your time, I'm afraid we'll run out of topics fast," I joke as I spin the fork to hook pasta onto it.

"Don't worry. I'm a man of many interests," Sean flashes me a lopsided smile. "Besides, I already have a topic in mind."

"Oh yeah? Which one?"

He stabs a piece of steak onto the fork and raises it to his lips.

"You," he says as he puts the meat into his mouth.

At this point, I can honestly say I'm beyond flattered to be a topic of interest for a guy like Sean. It's all I can do to suppress the smile that tickles the corners of my lips.

"Is that so?" I ask as I continue to rotate the fork.

More than a mouthful of pasta is on it, but I'm not focused on the food anymore. Sean chews, swallows, then takes a sip of water. All the while, he's not taking his eyes off of me, but it's not a creepy gaze like he's undressing me with his eyes. It's more of a look of admiration if I've ever seen one. It makes me feel like a queen.

Even more, it makes me feel like a goddess.

"I'm going to be honest with you. You intrigued me a lot on Tinder. In person, you're even more interesting," he says.

"Thank you," I say because I don't know what else to say.

I hope my cheeks aren't blushing. Something tells me they are. I quickly avert my gaze back to my plate, but I can feel Sean's eyes lingering on me. I suppress the urge to tell him the feeling is mutual. I'm *very* interested in him, but I don't want to show it just yet, not only because I'm afraid of coming off as too clingy but because I want to have the upper hand.

Sean has shown me his cards. Mine are still hidden. Maybe a rotten tactic, but I've been burned enough times before to know how to do things the safe way... sort of.

"I didn't take you for a shy person," Sean says.

"Shy?" I ask.

When I look up, he has a wry grin on his face.

"Yeah." He nods. "Over chat, you came off as..." He looks to the side as if carefully contemplating his words.

"Loud mouth?" I ask.

He looks at me, and I can tell I hit the nail on the head.

"I wouldn't call it that," he says.

"Well, you asked me out, so I'm assuming you either really like loud girls or you saw a redeeming quality in me."

I take a sip of wine. He smiles but doesn't answer.

"Anyway, I'm not shy," I add.

I don't take offense to people calling me shy or quiet. It's no secret that I'm no extrovert and that I prefer sitting at home on a Friday night watching a movie in my PJs than going out to a nightclub that reeks of alcohol and smoke and is crowded to the brim.

Come to think of it, I have no idea what Sean's preference is, and I'm suddenly interested to know. It's a big factor for me, believe it or not.

Please, God, don't let him be one of those people who like to party hard every weekend and then go out to meet with friends as soon as he sobers up. If that's the case, then we would need to make compromises in our relationship.

I would have to sacrifice my peace and quiet to go out and party with him from time to time, and he would need to lay off drinking every now and again to spend "us" time on the living room couch. That's going to end up with one side holding a grudge against the other.

No, I'm thinking about my ex. He was like that. Sean doesn't seem that way. He seems like the type who would gladly sit at home with me even though his friends invited him out.

Why am I getting way ahead of myself like this?

"What do you do on the weekends? Surely your company gives you time off from time to time, right?" I ask.

"I don't work on the weekends. I used to, but then I decided to focus on my work-life balance. They used to call me on Saturdays and Sundays to tell me to check my email or respond to this or that client. And the craziest part about all of that is I actually did it. Can you believe that?"

"Shockingly, I can," I say.

It's no secret that putting in overtime while working in corporate America is no longer a bonus—it's a basic requirement. You can decline to respond outside of your working hours, but they're just going to find somebody else who's willing to sacrifice their personal time for the company.

The trend called "quiet quitting" took off for a while, where people gave their bare minimum enough not to get fired, and it made me happy to see that the overworked and underpaid employees were finally standing up to their corporate overlords.

I'm glad to hear Sean values his private time. Like he said himself: Money is important, but time is something none of us will ever get back.

"And the company didn't give you trouble for it?" I ask.

"No. They need people like me. It might seem easy for companies to hire somebody new—and for some of them, it is—but in reality, training new hires is a hassle."

"So, since you have the free time on the weekends, what do you do to unwind from work?"

"Depends on how I feel that particular day."

"Do you go out anywhere?"

I hope my question doesn't sound too pushy, but I really want to know, not just whether he's a partygoer but also whether he's a people person. Not that there's anything bad with being a people person, but I just really want to find someone who hates socializing as much as I do.

I've had the displeasure of finding out what it's like to date an extrovert as an introvert, and it's not pretty for either side.

"Actually, I don't drink. I mean I do on rare occasions like these, but I don't do it to get drunk," Sean says.

Yes!

"That doesn't mean you can't go out, right?"

"Sure, and I tried going out when I was younger. Like, I really, really tried, but I could never have fun. Maybe my dad was right that going out and not drinking is like buying a car and not driving it."

"Did he really say that?"

"No. His version was a lot more vulgar."

I let out a peal of laughter at that. I'm interested to know how the original saying goes, but I don't push Sean for it.

"I know it might sound crazy, but I prefer quiet evenings. Like, I'm okay hanging out at home with a group of people playing board games or something, but going out..." He shakes his head. "I sound like an old person, I know."

You sound perfect, I want to say.

I can't wipe the grin off my face.

"I don't mind quiet evenings," I say as I rotate the glass of wine in my hand. "Besides, as long as I'm with the right person, it can turn into a loud evening quickly."

Jesus. What the hell are you saying, Melissa?

My cheeks burn from embarrassment. I quickly hide behind the glass, ready to take a sip until I remember that it must be the wine that has made me say what I just said.

I put the glass down and clear my throat. I'm afraid to look at Sean out of fear I'd see a judgmental glare in his eyes. Or worse, disgust. I must have come off as a slut, and that's not how my parents raised me, no sir.

I respect myself and my body, so that's why I'm so surprised at suddenly wanting to throw myself at Sean, tear off his clothes, and—

Keep it together, Melissa.

"I agree," Sean says, and I feel as though a boulder has fallen off my shoulders.

"Oh?" I ask.

"Yes. You know, I've never been the kind of person who follows logic," he says as he briefly looks down at his now-empty plate.

"That's strange, coming from a marketing expert. I thought you were all about numbers." I brush a bang from my face.

"You'd think so, but everything in life that I've done, I've done by listening to my feelings."

"How does that work? I mean, how do you know you're doing the right thing?"

"You're going to think I'm crazy if I tell you."

"Try me."

He leans over the table, and I can smell his Tom Ford perfume more prominently. "It's as simple as math. Simpler, even. Sometimes, when I look at something, I get this feeling. Call it a gut feeling or an instinct. I don't really know what it is. But if it tells me to go one way, I know it's the right way to go. It's like we have a symbiotic relationship—it steers me in the right direction like a compass, and I'm the one who gets us there."

He clears his throat and looks away for a moment as if embarrassed by what he's just said. "Does that sound stupid?"

I lean on my elbow, entranced by Sean's words. "No. Not stupid at all. And this helps you with work?"

What I really want to ask is: Does this also help you determine the right partner for you? I'm assuming I already know the answer. I've known it all night long. I can see the way he's devouring me with his eyes. That's not the way you look at someone you don't like.

"It's not restricted only to telling me whether a client would be a good fit for the company or not. It helps me with pretty much everything. In fact, I've found that it works wonders in helping me determine who I should add to my life."

His last sentence lowers to a whisper, and I find it strangely erotic. It must be the wine, so I put the glass down again. I don't even remember when I picked it up.

"I don't know if I'd be able to live my life like that," I say. "I'd be in constant fear of messing something up."

"Try it sometimes," he says. "Give in to the feeling without thinking about the risks or consequences, and you'll find yourself feeling liberated."

I smile at Sean because I like the way his life sounds. By the time he gets the bill (He pays the bill after asking me if

I'm okay with that, which I find incredibly gentleman-like), I'm still thinking about his gut-feeling decision-making.

It must be nice to be able to rely on instinct like that. You don't even need to calculate anything. Just let your gut decide, and you make it happen. Simple, just like Sean said.

Some people are naturally good at those things. They can look at a place and immediately tell it's bad. They can sense they're being watched even though they don't see anyone. They can talk to someone for five minutes and determine what kind of a person it was.

I don't know if it's the logical part of us that makes those decisions and we just call it a "gut feeling" because we don't really know what it is, or if it's some kind of a sixth sense that some of us are more naturally attuned to.

I wish I could do something like that. Unfortunately, I'm a terrible reader of people.

"Thank you for taking me out, Sean. I had a wonderful time with you," I say, making sure to emphasize the *with you* part.

Standing in front of the restaurant facing Sean, I feel like a schoolgirl. I notice he's standing much closer to me than he did when we first met, and I still think it's too much distance.

"Thank you for letting me take you out," he says. "To tell you the truth, I was really nervous when I asked you on this date. I like to think I take rejection pretty well, but, for some reason, it was really important for me that I get a chance to meet you."

"Maybe that was your instinct as well," I half-joke.

"That was maybe half of it."

"What was the other half?"

"The fact that I really like you."

Somehow, he's standing even closer to me. I don't know when and how that happened. Have I inadvertently gotten closer to him while shifting my weight from one foot to the other? Has he done it in a subtle way?

I don't really care. I'm glad he's close. And we're inching closer as we gaze into each other's eyes. I feel his fingers gently on my hip as if probing to see if I'm okay with it. I do nothing to stop it. He's like a magnet, and I can't help but pull closer and closer to him until our faces are only inches apart.

I find myself remembering his words.

Try it sometimes. Give in to the feeling without thinking about the risks or consequences.

I do exactly that.

Our lips press together. I feel a surge of electrical pleasure coursing through my entire body, the epicenter being the spot Sean's lips are touching. Something inside of me loosens and releases, and I suddenly need more of Sean. I need to get closer to him, and even though our bodies are pressed together, it's not enough.

The kiss seems to last way too short, and by the time Sean pulls away, my face is still burning.

"It's still early. Would you like to come to my place for a cup of coffee?" Sean asks.

I don't even drink coffee, and I sure as heck wouldn't drink it in the evening, just a few hours before bedtime. The kiss with Sean will already be more than enough to keep me up all night. The extra caffeine would only make things worse.

But this isn't about coffee. Coffee is just an excuse. A catalyst, if you will.

I take my time thinking over because, as much as I'm tempted, something tells me to slow down. Then I realize that's not happening. I know I'm rushing, but I've already made up my mind about going home with Sean.

The decision surprises me because I prefer taking things cautiously, but I'm seeing too many good things about Sean to pass this up.

Besides, this is only our first date. We can only take things so far. And as I said before, I'm a person who worries about tomorrow in the morning.

"I don't drink coffee, but I'd love to see your place," I say.

A smile crosses Sean's lips. He takes my hand and leads me to the spot where he parked his car. It's a fancy BMW, but I can't tell what kind exactly. I just say it's fancy because it looks fancy.

Like a real gentleman, Sean opens the door for me, and I slip inside. My heart is still pounding, and my cheeks burn. I'm sure it has nothing to do with physical exertion or the temperature.

Sean steps inside and starts the car. He flashes me another smile. I smile back.

I'm about to find out just how terrible I really am at reading people.

Chapter 4

"How long have you been teaching?" Sean asks.

"Three years. I've been trying to look for a job in another school, but it's really difficult finding a job as a teacher or teaching assistant nowadays," I say.

"I know a guy who works at Parkrose Elementary. He's actually the principal there. If you like, I can see if he can't get an interview for you. He owes me for a successful marketing campaign I ran for him."

"Really?"

I'm not sure how I feel about this. On the one hand, I would love nothing more than to work at Parkrose Elementary, and I'm incredibly flattered Sean offers to help me get my foot in the door. It's one of the more prestigious schools I've been eyeing for a while for a job opening. On the other hand, agreeing to let Sean help me would mean I would owe him, and I didn't know Sean nearly well enough to decide whether I could ask for such a favor of him.

"Yeah. Just say the word, and I can talk to him. I can't promise you'll get hired, but I'm sure he can push your resume to the front, if nothing else," Sean says. He focuses on the road for a second, then quickly adds, "I mean, if you want. No pressure."

"Thank you," I say and leave it at that.

I think that's a pretty reasonable way of handling it. I don't say no, and I don't say yes. I say "thank you," which means I'll get back to him if and when I feel that the time is right.

Five minutes of driving later and I notice how desolate the roads are. We're one of the only cars in the street. It suddenly occurs to me that I got in a car with a complete stranger who's taking me to his place, which I don't even know the location of.

I don't worry too much, though. I already told my roommate where I'm going, and I showed her the Tinder profile of who I'm going out with. Aside from that, Rachel forced me to install a tracking app so she could tell where I am at all times.

A single girl in her twenties can never be too safe nowadays, Rachel always says.

She also wanted me to take her revolver, which I thought was a little extreme.

I agreed to the tracking app but refused to touch the firearm. Rachel may be stubborn, but I am even more so when it comes to using loaded firearms.

Now that I'm in Sean's car, I feel a pang of relief that I ended up agreeing to install the tracking app. But Sean wouldn't do anything to me. He has shown me his face, and I know his full name. Someone as smart and successful as Sean didn't fit the profile of being a serial killer or anything like that.

"Where do you live?" I ask.

"Broadside," he says. "I bought a house there about a year ago."

Fancy neighborhood. If he managed to buy his own place in that neighborhood, it means he's doing really well with money. Compared to his, my place is tiny. I share a two-bedroom apartment with Rachel, and we barely manage to pay the rent and bills and have enough money to survive until the next paycheck.

My self-doubt increases when he parks his car in the driveway of an enormous house. My jaw figuratively drops to the floor when I see the huge fence and the statue on the fountain in the middle of the yard. It's like a mansion. The only thing missing is the hedge maze.

"You live here?" I ask.

I feel guilty because I don't want Sean to think I'm a gold digger, which would be an easy conclusion for him to reach.

In my defense, I'm not out actively looking for rich guys earning six figures. I didn't even know what Sean did for a living before tonight.

"Yeah. I'm not proud of too many things, but this house... it took a lot of planning in order to make it look like this," he says.

"You designed the house?"

"God, no. I am terrible at those things." He laughs. "I just gave the architect my idea, and he made it happen. Come on, let's go inside."

My eyes are still plastered to the house. The car is off, the absence of the engine amplifying our voices.

"What's wrong?" Sean asks.

He's already outside of the car with one foot, staring at me expectantly.

"Um, nothing," I blurt, but it's a lie.

Those gates mark more than just the border between public and private property. They mark the separation between a safe zone and a not-so-safe zone. But the front of Sean's house is not so safe, either, is it? If Sean wanted to do something bad to me, I could jump out of the car right now and scream, and someone would come help me.

Once I'm in there, though? Going to be a little harder to call for help.

Sean's hand on my thigh snaps me out of my thoughts.

"We don't have to do this if you're uncomfortable, Melissa," he says. "Just say the word, and I'll take you home."

That is more than enough to dispel any doubts I have in my mind. I squeeze his hand and smile, reassured.

"No, I'm good," I say. "I mean unless *you've* changed your mind."

"Never." He shakes his head.

We step outside. It's a little chilly. Sean unlocks the large, metallic gate, and holds it open for me. A minute ago, that door would have looked to me like cell bars. Sean's reassuring smile doesn't make me even consider that possibility.

I approach the gate then spin to take a look at the neighborhood. I consider how peaceful it looks.

Then, I step toward the house.

Chapter 5

Sean's house is as ostentatious inside as it is outside. His taste is unique and definitely not something I'd have in my own place (If I ever manage to afford it), but I have to appreciate the effort he put into it.

The walls have Victorian-style decorations on them, the protruding kind that depict pillars and other architectural things. You'd expect old furniture to go with those kinds of walls, but Sean has somehow managed to fit the modern with the old, and it looks amazing.

He offers to take my jacket, and I'm once again astounded and what a gentleman he is.

"Make yourself at home," he says as he gestures to the living room.

He makes his way behind the kitchen counter. On the wall behind him is an array of expensive-looking drinks under purple neon lights. I wonder if those are there just as decoration or if he plans on cracking them open on a special occasion.

"What would you like to drink?" he asks.

"I don't know. Actually, can I get something non-alcoholic?" I ask.

I'm already feeling the effects of the wine on me, and I don't want to make it worse.

"Of course. I got some soda in the mini-fridge," he says.

"Sure."

I feel my phone vibrate inside my purse. A wave of dread washes over me as I consider it might be Joshua from a different number. I rummage through my purse and pull my phone out. Rachel is calling me.

"Your roommate worried again?" Sean asks.

I see him staring toward me from behind the counter.

"Yeah. I'm just going to take this call real quick," I tell him.

"Go ahead," he says.

I drag the green button to answer. Immediately, Rachel's worried, crow-like voice jabs my ear.

"Where the hell are you? The locator shows you way off course."

"Don't worry. I'm with Sean. We went back to his place for some drinks."

Instantly, her combative attitude drops.

"Oh," she says, and then one more time in realization, higher-pitched. "Oh!"

"Yeah," I say.

"I am dying to know the details. Did the date go okay? Is he good-looking? Are you guys going to get naughty tonight?"

I look toward Sean to see whether he shows any signs of having heard the conversation. He's busy doing something around the kitchen, not paying attention to me. Rachel is not on speaker, but she talks loudly, so I wouldn't be surprised if Sean overheard her.

"Rach, listen. I'll let you know how things go when I'm home."

"When are you coming home?"

"I don't know."

"You'll be staying the night over there, won't you?"

"I don't know, Rach." I can see Sean coming into the living room. "Rach, I have to go. We'll talk later, okay?"

Before Rachel can say anything, I hang up. I'm eternally grateful for her being so caring, but boy, does she know how to prolong a conversation.

Sean comes with two cans of coke and sits next to me. He hands me one can.

"Thank you," I say.

I pop open the can. The drink fizzes and goes silent. I take a sip. It's refreshing.

"Your place is gorgeous," I say.

"Thanks, but I didn't put nearly as much effort here as I did into the library," Sean responds.

"You have a library?"

"Yeah. Want to see it?"

I'm not much of a reader, if I'm being honest. The last book I read was two years ago, and it was a 100-page self-help book about improving sleep. Still, though, whether you're a reader or not, you never say no to a host offering to show you their personal library. That would be disrespectful.

"Sure," I say.

We put our drinks on the table, and he leads me past the living room toward the door on the other side. He twists the knob, opens the door, and steps aside for me to go in first.

The flooring is different in here. It's wood flooring, just like in the living room, but it feels... older, if that makes sense. Not worn-down, rotted, or with planks hanging loose when you step on them, but rather as if the designer specifically went for something that looked old but felt new.

And, boy, does it go well with the rest of the room.

The tall ceiling stretches up to the top of the second floor. Rows and rows of shelves filled with thousands of books line every wall. There's a spiral staircase leading up to a catwalk on the second floor where more shelves sit.

On the bottom floor, there's a reading corner. It consists of comfy sofas, a fireplace, an ornate oak desk, and a sturdy chair. On top of the desk is a laptop. It's the only thing in the room that lets me know we're still in the twenty-first century.

"Oh my God," I say in awe.

It feels as though I've stepped into a place you need to pay $50 to get a thirty-minute tour of. Except there are no tourists here hoarding spots you want to take pictures of, and you have the entire place to yourself, and it's so beautifully quiet.

This room is every bookworm's dream. I instantly think about Rachel, who has a large bookshelf in our apartment that she's proud of. Her only bookshelf is smaller than one of Sean's. If she could see this place, she'd freak out.

I take out my phone. "Sean, do you mind if I take a picture to send to my roommate?"

"Actually, I'd prefer you don't do that," he says.

He looks uncomfortable after telling me that.

"Oh." My enthusiasm is instantly deflated.

The way I had taken my phone out, sure that Sean was going to give me the green light because he's so nice, makes me feel embarrassed about myself.

"I'm sorry," he says, even though it's not his fault.

"No, yeah. I totally get it." I nod as I stuff my phone back into my purse. "It's easy to forget that there are places that should not be looked at through the lens of a camera."

"It's just that I consider this room to be very private. It's my safe space. You know?" he says, which is an attempt to make me feel better.

"Oh yeah?" I ask as I step closer to him. "And do you show it to all the girls you take home?"

I playfully run a hand down his chest.

"Only to the ones I feel I can trust," he says, and it's the most right thing he can say in that moment.

We lean closer to each other, and our lips meet. Kissing Sean in the privacy of an enormous library is so much better than kissing him in the street in front of a restaurant. With no one watching, I feel more relaxed.

I can tell Sean feels the same way because of the way he puts his hand on my lower back and reels me closer, and the way his fingers gently slide up my arm toward my cheek. The air is heavy with romantic and erotic static.

For a moment, I think we're going to rip each other's clothes off and do it right there on the library floor. I can't help but wonder if he's already had sex with someone in here. The pang of jealousy that I'm not supposed to feel is stifled by Sean's kiss to my neck.

That's my sweet spot, and he seems to know this. Then again, my moans aren't very subtle.

I hear vibrating in the room. It doesn't take me more than a second to understand what it is. In an age where our faces are practically glued to our cellphones, we learn to recognize what every kind of vibration or ping stands for. The continuous vibrating that comes from Sean's pocket tells me someone is calling him.

When our lips part, we're both out of breath. Sean apologizes and reaches into his pocket.

I happen to glance at his screen and I notice the name Anna.

Another wave of jealousy hits me, this one stronger and more unpleasant than the one before. A part of me wants to storm out of the house. I knew this was all too good to be true. Sean is already seeing someone. Well, of course he is.

He is a ten. Chicks would be all over him. It doesn't justify him being a cheater, though.

He declines the call.

With it, my jealousy drops, and I start to think more rationally. I justify in my mind that Anna is just a friend or a colleague. I then stop and consider how psychotic I sound. Anna could be anyone, and I'm ruining the moment by immediately assuming that she's Sean's girlfriend.

Can you blame me, though?

Joshua cheated on me more than once, and it's made me hyper-sensitive to anything that may allude to infidelity. It was my own fault for taking him back after the first time he cheated on me. At least, I didn't stick around after the second time it happened.

I want to tell Sean that maybe he should have taken the call, but I'm too selfish for that. The moment his phone is back in his pocket, I'm all over him.

We can't keep our hands to ourselves on the way to the bedroom upstairs. By the time he throws me on the bed and starts undoing my bra, any doubts I had about Sean are gone. Either the paranoid part of me realizes that I've been irrational, or it's completely silenced by my desire to be with this handsome man.

"You're beautiful," he whispers into my ear and, right now, I feel exactly like that.

I see his eyes exploring me, admiring me, giving me that same look from before as if I'm a goddess. It makes me feel so powerful, so deserving—something I haven't felt in a long time. The final threads of reservation that I don't even realize were there are snapping.

I give myself to him completely, and he does the same for me.

Chapter 6

An hour later, Sean and I are lying in bed. He's on his back, and I'm leaning my head against his chest. The room smells of sweat mixed with his cologne. The sex was as amazing as I expected it to be, and now we're talking.

"When do you go to work tomorrow?" I ask.

"Not before eleven. You?"

"I have a day off tomorrow," I say.

He turns his head toward me. "Then you have no excuse not to stay tonight."

I'll admit I thought about it on the drive to his house. I knew we'd end up in bed, but I wasn't sure if he'd want me gone by the morning. Now I know he didn't want just a one-night stand.

"I don't want to intrude," I tell him, but a part of me is gauging whether he really wants me to stay.

He kisses my forehead. "Stay. I'll make you breakfast in the morning and drive you home."

He gets up and starts kissing me. He throws the sheet off and rolls over to be on top.

Somebody's eager, I think to myself as I run my hand through his hair.

The moment of romance is interrupted when the vibrating starts again. We continue kissing, but the sound is incessant.

"Sean..." I say between kisses.

You should get that, I want to say, but I just can't seem to pull away from him.

Each vibration trills in my head until I can't take it anymore. It feels like it lasts and entire minute before I pull back, my hand firmly on Sean's chest. He stops kissing me and looks at me with concern in his eyes, as if he might have accidentally hurt me.

"It sounds like it might be important. You should take it," I say.

"I'll call them later." He leans toward me, but I stop him.

"Sean, your friend obviously needs you. Go ahead and take the call."

His eyes drift to the floor where his pants are lying in a crumpled heap, then back to me. He looks like he's contemplating whether to listen to me or not.

I put my hands on his face and say, "Go. I'll be here."

Sean stands up and lets out an exasperated sigh. He puts on his underwear, picks up his pants, fishes his phone out—which is still ringing—and says, "Do not move. Stay exactly like that. I'll be here in less than a minute."

I flash him a smile and watch as he leaves the room. I hate detaching from him, but this call is obviously important if the person on the line would be willing to let it ring for over a minute.

"I'll be right back," he says before closing the door.

Only then do I hear his muffled speaking, but I can't discern the words. I don't care, really. I'm just eager for him to get back. I'm admiring the simplistic design of his bedroom as I listen to the voice outside the room. I'm incredibly turned on by his voice, I suddenly realize.

Since I have time to kill, I stand and walk over to the bathroom. On my way there, I accidentally rattle the nightstand and almost topple an ornamental vase on the floor. My hands are already stretched out to catch it, but the vase stops tottering and stabilizes.

Jesus, I think to myself.

I'd seen it earlier, and I almost knocked it down a few times during sex. Why does Sean keep such an expensive thing in here? I'll have to ask him to remove it while I'm around. I can't even imagine the damage it would do to my wallet if I broke it.

I enter the bathroom connected to the bedroom. I look at my ruined makeup and disheveled hair in the mirror and fix them as much as I can. As I'm doing that, my eyes fall on something that instantly catches my attention.

I turn around and walk up to the bathtub, on the side of which I see a bunch of products lined up. My brain refuses to believe what I'm seeing is really there. Denial can be one hell of a thing.

I pick up the pink bottle and stare at the women's shampoo.

Chapter 7

My eyes must be deceiving me, I think, so I rifle through the other products. The shampoo isn't the only one used by women. Some of these products are the ones I use at home. My mind races, and I'm too angry to believe I've been duped like this.

That bastard.

In my carelessness, I knock one exfoliating scrub into the bathtub. It slides down the slope with a loud clatter. I instinctively snap at the door, expecting to see Sean coming in to confirm whether I'm okay. When that doesn't happen for twenty seconds or so, I put the products back where they were and walk out into the bedroom.

At this point, I'm fuming. I want to burst through the door and call Sean all sorts of names before storming out. I'm putting on my bra and panties when I pick up on the faint hint of concern in Sean's voice. I then remember seeing the name Anna on the screen.

Anna.

She must be his girlfriend or wife. Of course there was a freaking catch. Of course there was. No way I can land a break and find a decent guy. I'm so angry at myself, and at Sean, and at Rachel for being so rightfully cautious, and at Joshua for making me lose my trust in people.

Sean's voice vacillates between raised and lowered, and I'm now sure there's a problem. I know I shouldn't, but I tiptoe to the door and lean my ear closer to it. I'm sure I'm going to overhear a conversation I'm not supposed to.

I'm able to discern more of what Sean is saying from here.

"Yes," his muffled voice comes from the other side of the door. "Yes. Okay, I get it. No, you have nothing to worry about. Everything is okay. I promise, everything is fine. Okay. I love you, too."

My heart jumps into my throat. Did I hear that right just now? Did he just tell the person on the phone that he loves her?

That's it. That seals it. I am out of here.

I pick up my clothes just as the door behind me opens. I suddenly feel vulnerable and used, standing in nothing but my bra and panties in front of Sean. Sure, he's only covered by his underwear, too, but that's different. He's a man.

"What's going on?" he asks.

What's going on, I want to parrot him in ridicule, but I'm too angry to even do that.

"I'm going home," I say.

"What? Why?" he asks.

He looks utterly shocked. What a great actor.

"Because you didn't tell me you're already seeing someone," I retort.

"What?" he asks again.

I clumsily slither into my jeans and button them up. I snatch up the crumpled blouse off the floor.

"Melissa, where's this coming from? Talk to me."

I want to slap him for patronizing me like that.

"Oh, don't play dumb. I heard what you just said to that person on the phone. And I saw the women's products in your bathroom." I point to the bathroom as if it's not already obvious enough.

Sean's head slumps, and he closes his eyes.

"Melissa, I can explain everything. Just give me a minute of your time," he says.

"There's nothing to talk about," I disagree.

I start toward the door, but Sean blocks my path. That is the second time tonight that a feeling of unease washes over me, and it's much stronger than the first one. It's the first time I realize—really realize—just how right Rachel was to take so many precautions.

Sean is much stronger than me, and I'm stuck inside his house. If I scream, no one will hear me. My purse is downstairs, along with my phone. My location tracker is on, but I already texted Rachel I'd be going home with Sean, so she'll assume nothing is wrong.

Cold sweat breaks out on my skin. It feels as though my ribcage is closing in on my lungs, constricting my breathing.

"Melissa, please. Just one minute, and if you don't believe me, you can go. Please," Sean says.

I don't really have a choice. I could say no, but is he really going to let me go?

"Fine." I cross my arms.

Sean offers me a tentative smile as he walks over to the bed and sits on the edge. That, at least, is a good sign. He doesn't plan on keeping me captive here. I hold my crumpled blouse in my hands as I wait to hear what kind of a lie Sean is going to concoct.

I've already made up my mind I'm going home. Now I just want to give Sean the impression that I care. Actually, I *do* care, I suddenly realize. One thing I've always disliked about myself is being the kind of person who can't let things go.

Call me crazy, but I need to reach a conclusion for everything in life. If I walk out now, it'll be like turning off the TV in the middle of the movie and. I know that's how some things work in life, but it's something I can't help, kind of like an OCD person stepping on cracks.

"I know this looks really bad," Sean says.

"No, why would it? A person named Anna calls you all night long. Then I see her products in the bathroom, and then I hear you tell her you love her. A completely normal thing to experience on a first date."

"That's not—"

"Are you married? Did you go out of your way to remove any evidence of your wife and you just forgot about the shampoo?"

"No. That's not the case. I'm—"

"Christ, I don't even see a ring on your hand. I get that your marriage might be on the rocks, but you can't drag me into all of this. All you're doing that way is—"

"Anna is my sister," Sean interrupts me.

His sentence utterly silences me. My lips are parted, and I feel like I'm supposed to say something, but nothing comes out of my mouth. Sean and I stare at each other for what feels like an eternity.

"What?" I stammer out.

I'm not sure if I should feel like an idiot for not considering the possibility that Anna is a family member—or for believing such a simple explanation.

"Your sister?" I ask.

I still can't string more than a few words together.

"Yes. I have a sister," Sean says. "She lives a few hours away, and sometimes she comes for a visit. That's why I have those things in my bathroom. I didn't want to throw them out even though she doesn't come by often."

I hate myself for giving Sean the benefit of the doubt. I hate myself even more for the feeling of relief that envelops me.

I quickly replay whether I saw anything in the house that might hint at the fact that Sean lives here with a woman. As hard as I try, I can't find anything like that. Nothing in this house looks as if it's seen a woman's touch.

"For someone who doesn't visit often, she sure calls you a lot," I say. "And that doesn't explain why you referred to her as your male friend back at the restaurant."

I specifically remember that moment. He had said it was his friend checking up on him. I had told him it was okay if he wanted to call him back. *Him.* And then Sean said "he" calls him too often.

Sean opens his mouth then closes it, and I realize I caught him in a lie. I want to feel triumphant, but nothing about this feels like I'm winning.

"I don't like to talk about her a lot. I wish I could have avoided this whole thing, but it's a big misunderstanding, and I don't want to lose you because of it."

He says he doesn't want to lose me as if we've been dating for a long time. I ignore that as I wait for him to continue talking.

"Anna... has mental problems," Sean says.

My eyes widen in the realization that I've been wrong. I haven't caught him in a lie. I simply forced him to talk about something that makes him uncomfortable.

"Oh," is all I can mutter.

I want to ask what kind of mental problems Anna is facing and how severe they are, but Sean answers that question before I can ask.

"She has schizophrenia. It's pretty bad. She needs to take medication daily."

"Sean, I'm so sorry. I didn't... I shouldn't have..."

I feel so stupid. I'm not going to be surprised if Sean asks me to leave.

"It's okay. You couldn't have known." He hangs his head down.

He doesn't ask me to leave, and I'm overcome by the need to hold him, so I drop my blouse to the floor and sit on the bed next to him. I put my hand on his thigh, carefully watching his reaction. He puts his hand over mine, which is a good sign.

"I know I should have told you before we went out, but I really like you, and I didn't want to scare you with it. I used to be pretty open about it on my dates, but the moment I mentioned Anna, they either changed entirely or outright ghosted me."

I nod. The need to hold him intensifies, but I feel like he wants to talk about this more, so I just sit next to him and gently rub his hand.

"I got pretty tired of it. I got angry with Anna. There were these moments when I... God, this is going to sound awful..." He takes a moment to compose himself. "There were these moments when I hated her for being the way she is. So, one day, I chose to pretend Anna doesn't exist. I knew it's wrong, and I knew they'd leave the moment they found out, but it just felt so good to live in that illusion that I'm appreciated. You know?"

"I don't blame you for doing that. Those other girls were really selfish to leave you like that," I say.

He nods but doesn't say anything. I have a feeling he's fighting back tears.

"Are you the one who needs to take care of Anna?" I ask.

"I used to be. But when I got this job, I was able to afford a caretaker, so I bought her a house relatively far from here but close enough for me to go visit if needed. But I still have to check up on her almost daily to make sure she's okay and that she's taking her meds."

I feel terrible. I had accused this obviously selfless man, who has devoted his life to his sister, of being a cheater. I wonder what I would have been like if the roles were reversed, but it's impossible to say with certainty. I don't have any siblings, let alone any that suffer from mental problems.

"I'm sorry," Sean says. "I understand if you want to leave."

But I don't want to leave. I see a glint in his eyes. I feel connected to Sean even more than before. More than while we were rolling in bed, panting in each other's faces. He's baring his soul with me, exposing his vulnerabilities, his fears, and I like him so much more because of it.

I don't know about other girls, but I like an emotional man. It shows me he's human and capable of being compassionate. Other girls can keep those macho guys who are afraid of showing their soft side.

Before I know what I'm doing, I lean toward Sean and kiss him. He presses his face tightly against mine, and I can feel how much he needs that. I gently push him onto the bed and climb on top of him.

"I'm not going to leave you," I whisper into his ear.

Chapter 8

"If one of those stars were to explode, we wouldn't know it for years because that's how long it would take light to reach us," Sean says.

I'm resting my head on his shoulder, tracing a finger in a circle around his chest. Sean's fingers are gently caressing my back. The sleepiness is making it difficult for me to remember how we got to the conversation about exploding stars.

Oh, right. I remember now.

Just minutes ago, Sean had told me about one activity he enjoys thoroughly—watching.

"Watching?" I had asked.

Of course, the first and only thing my dirty mind could think of was something that would either require a restraining order or a soundproof bedroom.

"Yeah. You know, like stargazing," he had said.

"Oh," I said.

Truth be told, I still couldn't tell whether I was relieved or disappointed, but I did feel like an idiot for not thinking of literally anything else. People watch all sorts of things without being weirdos.

"Have you ever done that?" he had asked.

"Can't say that I have," I'd said. "I'm a pretty antsy person. I'd get bored fast."

Sean had laughed. "I do it all the time when I go camping—stare at the constellations or the craters on the moon. It's not just the sky, though. If you stare at anything long enough, it opens up to you and tells you its story. And maybe that story is subject to interpretation, but once that story is spilt to you, it's your story, and you can see it how you want to."

I have to admit I was taken aback to hear him talking like that. I didn't take Sean for someone who can appreciate the abstract, but it suddenly made me like him even more.

"I just find staring at stars scary," I'd replied but didn't say why.

The truth is, I see those little, bright dots, and I know they're millions of miles away, surrounded by nothing but darkness, and I suddenly feel like I can get sucked into that vast emptiness, forever lost.

It's terrifying to think about what's out there and how much bigger it is than all of us, and how we humans are tucked into this bubble of safety we call earth.

That's when Sean started telling me random facts about stars, and that's how we got to the point of me learning that we wouldn't know if a star exploded until it was already gone entirely.

If I'm being honest, my mind is not entirely hung up on space facts. I keep thinking about Sean's sister, Anna. I keep thinking about what a difficult life Sean has and how it must be hard for him to devote time elsewhere because he's already committed full-time to his sister.

My brain is already looking for ways to make this whole thing work. A voice in my head keeps telling me things will work out between me and Sean as long as I'm patient. Then there's the other voice, the little devil on my shoulder that keeps urging me to walk out that door the moment Sean falls asleep and never look back.

No, I won't do that. It's just a passing thought.

If I do that, I'll be like the other girls who left him. How would I ever be able to look at another guy on a date and tell him what I want in a man when I myself am selfish and unwilling to make sacrifices?

Sudden buzzing on the nightstand startles me out of my thoughts.

"Damn," Sean says with a sigh.

I no longer feel sleepy. I prop myself up on one elbow and brush the hair out of my face. I can see Sean isn't putting much effort into reaching for his phone, so I say, "If it's Anna, you should take it."

He gives me an "are you sure" look before fumbling for the phone on the nightstand. He squints at the screen and sits up.

"It's work," he says. "I should probably take this."

"Yeah, go ahead. I'm gonna go grab a drink downstairs if you don't mind," I say.

Sean is already on his feet and pulling his underwear up with one hand while holding his phone up to his ear with the other hand. "Yeah. Make yourself at home. You remember where the kitchen is, right?"

Before I can crack a joke about his house being like a maze because of its size, he's already speaking to the person on the other end of the line. I put on my panties. I don't want to bother with a bra, and my eyes happen to fall on a plain, white t-shirt strewn over the top of the chair sitting in the corner.

I grab it by the hem and pull myself into it. I can smell Sean on it, and it makes me like the shirt even more. Just to be sure I'm not crossing any boundaries, I face Sean to see if I have his approval to wear the t-shirt.

He's talking on the phone, but he notices me, and he stumbles with his words before regaining his composure. A smile forms on his lips, and I can see in his eyes that he wants to cross the distance between us and throw me on the bed again.

I'm flattered, to say the least. I can't remember the last time someone's looked at me like that. We all like to feel beautiful and wanted. I guess I just forgot what that feels like.

I wave at Sean and make sure to give him a good view of my rear as I walk out of the bedroom. I close the door behind myself so I can give him the needed privacy for his conversation.

I'm having trouble orienting myself despite my earlier attempt at joking that the house is like a maze. In my defense, though, I didn't really get to see my surroundings because Sean and I were making out like teens in puberty on our way up to the bedroom.

I'm now for the first time noticing doors on both sides that I haven't seen before. I want to peek behind each one, but it's not my house, and it would be inappropriate to snoop. I could ask Sean to give me a tour later, though... or in the morning.

I walk downstairs into the kitchen and ogle the drinks in the minibar. I don't feel like drinking something caffeinated that will keep me sleepy all night but prevent me from actually falling asleep, so I open the fridge instead and pull out a carton of OJ.

Strangely, I feel comfortable in the house. Not like I'm one hundred percent at home exactly—because I still have that precaution at the back of my mind not to knock something expensive like that vase in the bedroom over—but as close as it can feel to a home after spending a couple of hours in it.

I locate a glass and pour OJ into it. I return the carton to the fridge and take the first sip of the juice as I lean on the counter. After such strenuous activity in the bedroom, the cold beverage is refreshing. Sean's stamina is scary. I didn't think I could keep up with it, but he's able to evoke it out of me.

I pick up the glass off the counter and stroll into the living room, observing the details I hadn't had time to check out earlier because I was so focused on Sean. I feel as though I'm getting to know him better with each second I stare at a piece of furniture.

If you stare at anything long enough, it opens up to you and tells you its story, Sean had told me just minutes ago.

I take a seat in the exact same spot as when I first arrived. I put the glass of orange juice on the coffee table in front of me and rummage through my purse for my phone.

A message from Rachel.

Hey, how's it going?

Good! I reply. *I almost stormed out, though.*

Three little dots appear under my message to indicate Rachel is typing.

Oh no! Why?

Long story. Tell you in the morning, I type.

For a little while, Rachel doesn't respond, but then the dots appear on the screen again. They intermittently disappear and reappear, so I use that time to stand and approach one of the shelves. I check out the books Sean has lined up over there. Most of them are books on psychology, like getting rid of anxiety, controlling your thoughts, making friends, etc.

The fact that these books are in the living room and not the library must mean they're important to him. Maybe they helped him become who he is today.

I try to imagine Sean as a younger guy with self-esteem issues and shy talking to girls, but the image can't seem to enter my head. Maybe he's always been a charmer and he just wanted to improve what he already had.

I look down at my phone to see a new message from Rachel.

I told myself I wouldn't say this because I didn't want to ruin your date, but I'm a little skeptical about this whole thing, it says.

She'd already told me that just a few days ago, but she couldn't add any more information to that. After letting her think it through, she shrugged it off as her imagination.

We've been through this already, I send to her.

I know, I just can't shake the feeling. It's as if I expect something bad to happen. I dunno, she types.

You're probably just overthinking it. Anyway, I gotta go back. Talk to you tomorrow.

Laterzzzz.

But I don't go back upstairs right away even though I'm eager to return to Sean. Instead, I mindlessly tap on Facebook. I don't know why I did that. I think switching from one social media to another is pretty much a reflex at this point.

I lock my phone when I realize I've been scrolling past posts like a zombie for a few minutes. At this point, I'm just eager to get back upstairs to Sean.

You know what I really miss? Falling asleep in someone's arms. I know it may sound pathetic, but I'm really looking forward to that tonight.

I slide my phone into my pocket, except it falls through thin air and clatters on the floor because I have no pants. I look down in time to see it disappear under the bookshelf.

"Oh, shoot," I say as I get down to pick it up.

I reach for it, and then my eyes fall on something on the bottom shelf, nestled among the books.

A camera.

Chapter 9

It's not what you think.

It's not a spy camera placed in a way that the lens is staring at me. Besides, the bottom shelf would be the worst place for something like that.

No, this is just a digital camera like the one you'd take on your vacation to snap photos of landmarks and nature. I stare at it for a long time—the only reason I can tell it's been long is because the muscles in my legs are starting to burn from squatting.

If I'm being honest, the only reason I haven't reached for the camera is because of its positioning. It's not exactly hidden, but it's not out in the open, either. That tells me that Sean might not appreciate me touching his things without asking.

Curiosity roils inside me. I bite my lip as I weigh my options. I look toward the stairs, half-expecting to see Sean staring down at me with a scowl. No one is there, though, but I suddenly feel as though I'm doing something I shouldn't be caught doing.

As if even finding the camera has put me in that position.

I'm too drawn to the camera. Sean had mentioned earlier watching things, and I figure he must have some nice pictures on this camera. I suppress the thought that I might see some intimate pictures or videos over there that might make me jealous.

My fingers coil around the object, and I gently pull it out. By now, I have to stand because my legs are burning from the squatting. I locate the power button and press it, but nothing happens. My heart sinks at the thought that the battery is dead.

But then the camera's logo appears on the screen, and I'm overcome by a sense of excitement. At the same time, my heart is racing, and I glance at the stairs every now and again just to make sure Sean isn't there.

I then realize that I'll only look more guilty that way. If he catches me with the camera, I can just tell him I got curious and that it didn't occur to me that he might have some private things on there.

I enter the gallery, and the first picture pops up. It's a picture of a sunset above a lake. I'm not a photography expert, but the way the image is captured—the angle, the lighting, the filters, all that—looks pretty professional to me.

Pressing the button to move to the next picture, I find an image of treetops from a view below. The sun peers through the leaf-rich branches, and I consider what a good wallpaper this could make on a desktop.

I smile because I feel like I'm connecting with Sean through the camera, like I'm seeing an expressive part of him that can't be conveyed in words. A pang of worry hits me that I'm peering into his soul without his permission.

I move on to the next picture, and my smile drops.

It's a picture of a blonde woman posing in front of the camera. She's wearing a beanie and a scarf, and the tawny background tells me this picture was taken during fall.

I'm envious, and not just because she's beautiful but because she's posing like a model on the cover of a fashion magazine. The best I can do for a pic is a smile that doesn't come off as awkward, but even then, I have to focus on so many other things—the eyes, the eyebrows, the tension in the shoulders, the posture...

This chick, however? She is a natural.

I study the details of the woman, admiring her beauty, comparing them to myself. I'm starting to think this was a mistake. I can't look at her anymore. Despite that, I move on to the next picture.

It's another picture of her, but... no, wait, it isn't. It's a different blonde. This one's a full-body shot of a woman in a man's shirt, leaning against a wall and staring off into the distance. Just like the first woman, she is gorgeous. The next image shows the same woman, but she's lying in bed in sexy lingerie and looking at the camera upside down. She has a finger seductively in her mouth.

I tap the button, and the image changes to show a third woman. Like the other two, she's blonde, cute, but the way she stares at the camera doesn't give off the fashion magazine cover girl impression. It's more of a candid moment caught by the cameraman.

That's when jealousy really boils inside me. Why is Sean keeping these pictures?

And still, against my anger, I keep cycling through the pictures. Another one comes into view, another different blonde. And another. And another. And—

"Hey," a voice behind startles me so abruptly that I almost drop the camera.

I let out a small gasp as I spin to face Sean. He's smiling at me, but then his eyes gravitate to the camera in my hands, and his lips downturn. There's no way out of this for me. How do I even begin to explain that I was going through his photos?

"I... I was just..." I stammer, unable to form a proper excuse.

Before I know what's going on, Sean snatches the camera from my hands. He gives it a once over. He can see the last picture I left it on, and his face somersaults from disappointment to something akin to anger.

"Sean, I'm so sorry. I wasn't trying to—" I start.

"This has some private photos on it," he interrupts me.

"I just thought—"

"There's a reason why the camera was at the bottom where I left it."

"I know, I—"

"You probably wouldn't like it if I went poking around your things."

He's staring at me like he's about to throw me out.

"I'm really, really sorry. I didn't think this through. I just remembered that you said you like stargazing, and I wanted to see some of your pictures. I... I guess I felt as though I'd get to know you better that way."

Sean's eyeballing me as if deciding whether to believe me or not. Then, he smiles, and the tension in the air bursts like a bubble.

"I'm sorry. I didn't mean to snap," he says. "It's just... I'm a very private man, especially for my passion projects."

"No, I'm the one who should be apologizing. If I had known, I wouldn't have snooped. I'm sorry."

"It's okay. Forget about it," he says as he steps closer and gives me a peck on the forehead. "Are you hungry? What do you say we have a snack?"

He returns the camera to the bottom shelf and hands me my cellphone off the floor. I walk up to my purse and slip it inside.

"Sure," I say, and the world seems right again.

Except, it doesn't, because those blondes on Sean's camera have become imprinted in my mind's eye, and relief makes way for jealousy to manifest again.

"I'll make you a sandwich. What would you like in it? Actually, how about I surprise you? I make one hell of a sandwich."

"Um... sure." I shrug.

Sean's behind the kitchen counter, scooping up ingredients for the sandwich.

"Sean? Can I ask you a question?" I ask.

I know I'm already on thin ice, but being silent in my relationship with Joshua was what made things so bad. I was essentially his punching bag, and I'm not going to go through that again, even for a man like Sean.

Besides, we're still on our first date. Plenty of things could go wrong.

"Sure, what's up?" he asks.

I gulp twice before asking the next question. "Who are all those girls in the pictures?"

Sean's staring down at the piece of bread that he's spreading peanut butter over. He stops what he's doing, leans on the counter, and looks up at me. I once again feel small under his gaze, as if I've asked something terrible.

"Models," Sean says.

It takes my brain a moment to register the word.

"Models?" I repeat.

Sean resumes spreading peanut butter over the piece of bread. "Yeah. I sometimes pay aspiring models to take their photos."

"Like, you pay them to pose, and you take pictures?" I ask.
"Yeah."
"Oh."

He pauses with a grimace on his face, and I can tell he's unsure if he should have spoken up. He looks up at me and asks, "I'm sorry, is that weird?"

"No, not at all," I say. "I'm just taken aback is all."

"Are you... reconsidering this whole thing because of it?"

"What? No. Absolutely not. I just... I guess I thought they were your girlfriends, so I got kinda worked up." I let out a chuckle.

A part of me is just fishing to see what he will say. If he doesn't deny it, that's bad.

"No. They're just girls looking for modeling opportunities," Sean says. "It's really hard to come by that kind of work without prior experience, so I pay them for it. It's also super expensive to get professional models to pose for you. This way, I get the pictures cheap, and they get the experience they need. It's a win-win situation."

"So, do you do it often?"

Sean shrugs. "Once every couple of months. Sometimes more often. Depends what kind of photography I'm in the mood for."

"Right. Okay."

"Are you sure you're okay with that?"

"Yeah, totally."

The truth is, I'm not really sure how I feel about it. I want to be okay with it, but I have this nagging feeling that I can't get rid of.

"Melissa," Sean says my name sternly. "Are you absolutely sure?"

"Yeah, I'm sure, but..."

"It doesn't make you comfortable knowing I take pictures of half-naked girls, right?"

He hit the nail on the head, so I bite my lip.

"It's just some of those pictures look provocative," I say.

Sean stops focusing on the sandwiches again and looks at me. "Melissa, I don't look at those girls that way. I look at it as a hobby and a job. Besides, I rarely do those kinds of shots."

"I see."

"Hey, if it really does bother you so much, I'll just focus on nature."

The way he says it suddenly makes me realize what an awkward situation I've put him in. I don't want Sean to stop doing his hobby just because I'm uncomfortable with it. Sure, we're pretty much already dating, but I have no right to ask such a thing of him.

"No, I don't want you to stop something because of me," I say.

"It's just a stupid hobby anyway," Sean says. "Besides, you're more important to me."

It warms my heart to hear him say that.

"Okay, your sandwich is done, Your Majesty." He puts a plate with two pieces of bread stuck together on top of the counter.

From here, I can't tell what's in the sandwich, but I'm assuming it's PBJ.

"Thank you, good sir." I feign a clumsy bow and approach.

I observe the sandwich from multiple angles.

"What's in this?" I ask.

"It's a surprise," he says with a wink.

His sandwich is ready just in time for me to take the first bite. My mouth is flooded with flavors that I recognize as peanut butter, jelly, banana, cinnamon, and I think I'm detecting some traces of honey in there. I usually don't like when sandwiches have too many rich flavors, but this one hits the spot just right.

"Oh wow," I say with my mouth full.

"Good?"

"Really good."

We chew in silence for a little bit, but my mind keeps coming back to the pictures. I'm no longer bothered by it; just curious. I feel like there's no harm in talking about it anymore.

"By the way, why are all the girls there blonde?"

"I have a fetish for blondes," Sean says.

I recognize sarcasm in his tone but just barely, so I decide to play along.

"Is that why you hooked up with me? You want to take pictures of me for your collection?" I ask, twirling my finger around my hair.

"Yes. And when I'm done, I'll throw you in my basement with all the other girls I kidnapped."

I laugh.

Sean shakes his head. "No, I had different kinds of pictures in mind I wanted to take with you. Maybe even videos."

"I'm intrigued. Maybe you should bring that camera upstairs."

I'm only joking, so I hope he doesn't really take me up on that offer. If he does, I'll have to tell him I wasn't being serious. The last thing I need is for someone to have my sex tape that they can blackmail me with.

I may be rushing things with Sean, but I'm not stupid.

"I'm in the mood for a drink. You want one?" he asks.

"I could go for a glass of wine, I guess," I say.

"Lucky for you, I'm a man who's always prepared. I have some wine in the cellar. Let me finish up here, and I'll grab it."

"I can do it."

He raises his eyes toward me.

"I'm not going to snoop this time. I promise."

Sean smiles. "The cellar's just that way." He points to a door next to the stairs. "Don't forget to put on the slippers."

"You have a collection of wine just like you have books?" I ask.

"I'm afraid it's nowhere near as impressive as my library."

"I would hope so. Otherwise, I'd think you have a problem."

With that, I start toward the cellar door. Sean grabs me by the wrist and pulls me in for a kiss before letting me go.

"Just don't stay down there for too long; otherwise, you'll catch a cold," he shouts from the kitchen.

I love how caring he is. I can just picture him babying me when I'm feeling under the weather.

Next to the door is a pair of slippers. I slide my feet into them, open the door, and stare at the dark staircase descending into more darkness.

"The light switch is on the wall to your right!" Sean shouts.

I locate it and flick it up. Instantly, the entrance to the cellar is bathed in a bright light. I descend the steps, feeling a chill run down my exposed legs. The temperature here is a lot lower than the rest of the house. I'd better grab a bottle of wine and get out before I freeze to death.

I'm glad I have the slippers on because I can't imagine how icy my feet would have felt. When someone says the word "basement," I imagine a damp, dark, dirty room with cobwebs hanging off the ceiling. When someone says "cellar," I picture an equally dark place but filled with bottles of wine.

Sean's cellar is unlike either of those. When my feet touch the bottom of the stairs, I locate a second light switch and flip it on. The light that bathes the cellar is fit for a surgery room.

"Wow," I exclaim.

Sean was right, the cellar is nowhere near as impressive as his library, but it's still impressive. A lot of the bottle holders are empty, but I can see a bevy of drinks sticking out, waiting to be picked. On the far side of the room is a glass display with more wine bottles, ones that probably hold a higher monetary or sentimental value.

I decide not to approach the display out of fear of leaving smudges on the glass or, God forbid, breaking something. In fact, just standing here in the cellar makes me feel like I'm on eggshells. The chill that swaddled me earlier is now stronger, and it's telling me to get out. I want to grab a bottle and leave, but I also want to spend a minute admiring the collection.

How did Sean become so successful? Did he sell his soul to the devil or something? Wait, he's not secretly doing something illegal, is he? No, that's ridiculous. He's a hardworking businessman, that's all.

I want to believe that everyone can build a house like Sean's if they work hard enough, but then I remember my assistant teaching salary, and I realize you'd need to do something unconventional for that, like start your own business or whatever.

The cold has nestled into my body, making goosebumps break out on my skin. It's time to go.

I grab a bottle of red wine from 1990 and turn to leave.

That's when I hear a loud clatter upstairs. I pause, and the silence that ensues is deafening.

"Sean?" I call out but receive no answer.

Footsteps race throughout the house before receding.

"Are you okay?" I call out again, but there's no response.

He should have heard me, right? The door is open, and he's right there in the kitchen.

More footsteps, and then...

Then I hear the door of the cellar slamming shut.

CHAPTER 10

At first, I'm too stunned to move. My brain is racing, searching for reasons why the door might have shut.

It might have been the wind, I think, until I remember no windows were open.

Okay, then maybe Sean accidentally ran into it and it shut. But why was he running in the first place?

"Sean?" I call out, but there's no response.

The longer I stare at the closed door at the top of the stairs, the more I feel anxiety bubbling inside me, and I still don't understand why. All I know is my fingers and toes are numb from the cold, and I don't think it has anything to do with the temperature in the cellar.

"Sean!" I shout.

Even before waiting for his response, I put the bottle of wine on the floor—as gently as my growing panic allows me to—and race up the stairs. My eyes are fixed on the door at the top.

I stretch my hands out and grab the doorknob. I twist it, but nothing happens. In my frazzled state, I rattle the doorknob, thinking it might be stuck or something, but it refuses to budge.

That's when my chest starts tightening.

"Sean!" I call out, but my voice comes out meek.

"Sean!" I repeat as I bang on the door. "Sean, open the door!"

I jangle the handle again, then bang on the door, then call out to Sean, multiple times over, but the only thing that greets me on the other side is silence. I lean my ear against the door to listen, but my shallow breaths are making it impossible to hear anything—that, and the fact that the door is sturdy as hell.

"Sean! Let me out of here!" My cries are becoming more high-pitched.

I can't help it because of the vise-like emotions mounting against me. I just want out of this place. I feel as though the walls are closing in on me, and I'm hyperventilating. That lack of breath is what ultimately stops me from screaming.

I lean my forehead and palms against the door and focus on taking in deep and steady breaths. Just when I feel like the flow of air to my lungs is widening, the thoughts in my head go rampant, and my throat grows constricted again.

After I run out of every excuse in my head, I face the terrible truth that's been sitting right in front of me this entire time.

Sean has locked me in here. There's no other explanation. I desperately try to look for a different answer, but it all comes back to the same thing. Sean has lured me in here with this exact intention in mind—and I fell straight into his trap.

I even made it easy for him. How could I have been so stupid? I should have waited at least until the second date to go back to his place. I shouldn't have ignored all those red flags.

A sister with schizophrenia? Yeah, right. What a liar. I bet he doesn't even have a sister. And then there's that album full of blondes...

That's the one that really makes me panic. Who are those girls, and what did he do to them? Did he lock them in the cellar, too? I don't see any dead bodies or traces of struggle, so maybe he wasn't lying when he said they were just models.

Or maybe he just scrubbed the place clean after killing them, a voice in my head says, and I feel another wave of panic splashing me.

My thoughts drift to my purse. It's in the living room, along with my phone. Someone is bound to realize I'm missing. Rachel will call sooner or later.

Except, I told Rachel I'd talk to her in the morning, and morning is hours away. A million things could happen before then. He could kill me ten times over and no one would know what had happened to me.

The panic in my chest is so potent this time that I have to sit down. I hug my knees and rock back and forth. I can feel a wave of tears ready to pour out of my eyes, but I'm fighting that urge.

If I start crying now, I'll lull myself into a feeling of despair, and that would mean I've given up. I can't allow myself to do that. If I do that, I'll never see the outside of this cellar ever again. I have to stand up to Sean.

What does he plan on doing to me anyway? Keep me in here as his pet? That will never fly. Whatever he has in mind, it will never fly. Rachel knows where I went, so it won't be long before the police put two and two together. He's going to be arrested for kidnapping and... well, let's hope it's just kidnapping.

No, something is off about this whole thing. It seems like a rash move. It doesn't seem like something Sean would do. He's too intelligent for something that would immediately put him in the crosshairs of the authorities. That can only mean one thing.

Sean has found a way to do this without consequences.
Oh God... Oh God...

Am I the first person to fall for his charm? No, the girls in the photographs... they must have fallen victim to his deception, too. I once again reprimand myself for ignoring the red flags.

I look down at the bottle I left on the floor. I grab it by the neck and suddenly feel slightly empowered. I'm sure Sean has taken extra precautions to stop his victims from being able to escape, but that doesn't mean I'm just going to keel over and give up.

I approach the wall, squeeze the bottleneck with both hands, and swing the wine. I squeeze my eyes shut just before the bottle produces an ear-splitting sound of glass shattering. I open my eyes to see red liquid all over the wall and floor. Some of it has made it onto my slipper. The floor is interspersed with glass shards.

The broken bottle in my hand suddenly feels light, and I inspect the jagged edges to see how good of a weapon it would make. It's not ideal, but if I swing the thing right, I could do some serious damage. I just hope Sean doesn't have a gun because then my efforts will have been in vain.

I try out a few different grips on my new weapon and stab at the air, imagining Sean coming at me. It's a long shot, but if I hit his jugular or eye, I could buy myself enough time to sprint out of the house and flag a car down for help.

Maybe the thoughts of injuring Sean and making it out to safety are unrealistic, but it's all I have. It's the only thing keeping me from going insane.

I step away from the scattered glass and spilled wine and sit with my back against the wall, the weapon in my hand and poised for an attack.

Now, I wait.

Chapter 11

I'm shivering. I don't know how long I've been stuck down in the cellar, but I'm having difficulty keeping myself warm. Even pacing back and forth and rubbing my arms doesn't help anymore. If I stay here much longer, I might suffer from hypothermia by the time Sean pays me a visit.

That might be exactly what he's aiming for. He's wearing me down, keeping me cold and awake, and when I finally drop my guard, he's going to step inside and do whatever he's planned on doing.

But what could he want with me? I already had sex with him. I would have slept with him again if he only asked. Why go through so much trouble to lock me in his cellar?

The answer comes to me immediately.

To serial killers and rapists, it's not about the sex. They don't get pleasure from regular intercourse like the rest of the world. They get it from seeing their victims squirming, screaming, and begging for mercy.

Another jolt of panic envelops me, so I grip the broken bottle in my hand tighter. Strangely, it gives me comfort to do so. No matter how useless it might be as a weapon, at least I'm not unarmed.

I glance toward the wine-stained wall where I had broken the bottle. I look at the empty wine holders, and I wonder if the reason why the cellar is so empty is because other girls had the exact same idea as me.

If that's the case, then I'm already doomed. I try to tell myself that Sean simply forgot that I could use a broken bottle to defend myself, but I know deep down inside that's not true. He's very meticulous when it comes to everything else in life, so why would he stop here?

The cold is making it impossible for me to think. The faster I pace, the more the heat seems to leave my body. The more that happens, the more other, intrusive thoughts enter my mind.

I start to think that maybe this is all just a big misunderstanding. Maybe the door simply shut on accident and Sean can't hear me. Is the cellar soundproof even?

The right thing to do is wait for Sean to come inside so I can ambush him, but I can't take it in here anymore. I climb up the stairs and jangle the knob, hoping for a different result this time.

Still stuck.

I raise a hand to whack the door but then tell myself I will accomplish nothing by being hysterical. If Sean really did lock me in here, then he's reveling in my fear. I have to convince him that I'm not afraid anymore.

Gently, I rap on the door. "Sean, are you there?"

It takes everything in me not to shout at him to open this goddamn door. I press my lips tightly then call out again.

"Sean, if you can hear me, the door is stuck. I need you to open it. Please."

Nothing, and it only makes me want to scream even more. I stifle that urge and let out a sigh. I look down at the doorknob and consider the possibility of breaking the whole thing down. I immediately give up on that idea because the door is way too sturdy. Not only that, but even if I wanted to kick it down, I wouldn't be able to do so because it opens inward, and not outward.

Why do I have the feeling this was all built precisely like that for a reason?

But one thing doesn't make sense, though. I know one thing about Sean for sure, and that's that he's meticulous and calculated about everything—just like every serial killer. So then, why lock me in a wine cellar? You'd think that someone like him would have a dungeon specifically for victims like me.

Nothing about Sean makes sense anymore, and I start to think that bashing my head, thinking about it, will do me no good anyway. I walk down the stairs, defeated, my head hanging down. I want to lie down and sleep, but I know I can't allow myself to do such a thing.

I can't allow Sean to get the drop on me. I'm already helpless enough stuck in this cellar, but if I allow him to take away my weapon and bind me or something, I'll be completely and utterly at his mercy.

Those thoughts in my head hardly have time to finish manifesting when I hear something upstairs. Something like a shatter. I hear glass clinking against the floor. Some footsteps, and then I hear the scariest and most beautiful sound in the world.

The sound of the door's lock clicking.

I freeze, my heart thumping against my ribcage. Did I really hear that just now, or did my desperate mind conjure up that thought? I twist and look up toward the door. A sliver of light falls through the now-open crack, which confirms that I haven't imagined it.

I'm so stumped that all I can do is stare as the crack of the door widens, widens, widens. I can see a shadow standing in the doorway, revealed inch by inch.

Run, you idiot. Run.

That's enough to spur me into action. I duck behind the corner, back against the wall, the bottle held firmly in both hands. Well, as firmly as their violent shaking allows me to hold it.

Then, I hear the distinct sound of footsteps coming down the stairs, and I gulp against the urge to whimper.

Pull yourself together, Melissa. It's now or never. This is a crucial moment. If you mess this up...

The footsteps draw closer. I hold my breath because I don't want to give away my location. Not like there are many places to hide here, but Sean would need to look left and right to see where I am. I'm hoping he looks the wrong way first so I can stab him with the bottle.

Step. Step. Step.

Am I even going to be capable of causing physical harm to Sean, or will I freeze? I have to keep telling myself he won't hesitate to hurt me, so I have to show him the same courtesy.

The footsteps are almost upon me. I can see Sean's shadow on the floor, growing taller and taller. I'm squeezing the wine bottle so tightly my hands are cramping up. Just a little longer.

Sean emerges in front of me. He's facing forward, a look of confusion on his face. I think nothing of it despite the nibble of doubt that makes its way into my mind. I've already raised the bottle above my head, and I'm ready to bring it down.

Sean must have either heard me or noticed my presence because his head snaps toward me. His eyes widen, and he takes a step back, a hand raised in front of him defensively.

"Wait!" he shouts.

And I do. I don't know why. Is it the fear in his eyes? Is it because I can't bring myself to kill another human?

No matter how loudly the voice in my head screams at me not to show him mercy, I can't do it. And in the end, it's a good thing I don't listen to it.

Because standing in front of me is not Sean.

It's Joshua.

Chapter 12

My mouth works, forming wordless shapes, because I can't find anything in the English language to express myself.

"Melissa!" Joshua exclaims. "You're okay!"

You're okay?

What's that supposed to mean? What's he doing here? I am so confused right now.

"What?" That's all I manage in my discombobulated state.

Before I could say or think anything else, Joshua leaps toward me and embraces me in a tight hug. That's when things slowly start to make sense finally. I feel myself relaxing against his body, and I allow the bottle in my hand to slip from my grip. It clatters to the floor. In the absence of any other noise, it sounds deafening.

I only vaguely realize that I'm crying. Joshua is the last man I want to be held by—well, actually, Sean beats him by a little—but I can't help but feel relieved that I see another person down in the cellar. Not only am I not alone, but the person in front of me is the man I used to trust wholly. The man who had promised to shield me from all the bad in the world.

The man who had lied.

That sudden realization makes me snap out of my stupor. I push myself away from him and wipe my tears.

"What are you doing here, Josh?" I ask.

"I came to save you. I heard you were in trouble, so here I am," he says.

"What? What does that even mean?"

"There's no time. I'll tell you everything later. Right now, we need to get out of here and call the police. Come on."

I open my mouth to protest, but Joshua is already pulling me upstairs. I don't mind. I just want to be as far away from this place as possible. I can't express how happy I am to see the bright lights in the living room. But I'm still feeling uneasy. I'll keep feeling this way until I'm out of this house and as far away from this neighborhood as possible.

I scan the living room but see no signs of Sean.

"Where's Sean?" I ask.

"I knocked him out. He's in the kitchen," Joshua says as he keeps pulling me. "Hurry up, we need to get out of here."

I then remember that my purse is still in the living room. I can't leave it there. As much as I want to put distance to this house, I don't want to give myself any more unnecessary headaches.

"Wait, Josh," I say. "I need to get my things."

"There's no time," he says as he pulls me toward the door.

I glue my feet to the floor and say, "My purse is right there. I'll be right back."

"Melissa..."

"Just give me a second."

He stares at me as if contemplating whether to let me go or not.

"Fine," he finally says as he releases his grip on my wrist.

I stride into the living room, keeping my eye on the kitchen. There, I see Sean splayed on the floor, unconscious. A rivulet of blood coats the corner of his forehead, and some of the expensive-looking liquor bottles lie shattered on the floor next to him.

I realize I've been staring at Sean for too long when Joshua calls out to me.

"Did you get it?" he asks.

"Just a second," I say.

Still keeping my eyes plastered to Sean, I walk up to my purse—it's exactly where I had left it—and pick it up. I don't feel comfortable going out in nothing but my panties and Sean's t-shirt, but there's no way I'm going back upstairs to retrieve my clothes and risk getting locked in.

I rummage through my purse to look for my phone. That's the most valuable thing I have on me in a situation like this one. In case Sean comes after us, all I need to do is dial 911, and he's done for.

My fingers come in contact with the blocky outline of my cellphone, much to my relief. I pull it out of my purse and squeeze it in my hand. The screen lights up—I must have accidentally pressed a button—and I can see a bunch of notifications on it. I should wait until we're out to check them, but the three missed calls and five messages from Rachel convey a sense of urgency.

Rachel is naturally apprehensive about everything, but three calls and five messages in less than an hour is a lot, even for her. I can tell that whatever it is she wants, it's important. I open the text messages and read them line by line.

Dude, that tracking app we installed? Somebody else is using it.

Since I'm tracking you, I get a ping when someone else pinpoints your location. I just got a notification that someone did it. Turn it off right now.

Call me as soon as you can.

Where are you???

If you don't call me back soon, I'm calling the police.

A shiver runs down my spine as my eyes dart across each message. Somebody pinged my location. Somebody has been tracking me.

"Melissa!" Joshua's voice startles me, and I almost drop the phone.

He's standing right next to me, a look of impatience on his face.

"What are you doing? Let's go," he says.

I glance over at Sean's unconscious body. I see his eyes fluttering. He's waking up. We don't have much time.

"Joshua, how did you find me?" I ask.

"What?" he asks.

The frown on his face communicates ridicule, as if I just asked the stupidest question ever.

"I asked, how did you find me? How did you know I was here?"

"Does it really matter? Come on, Melissa. We need to get to the police before this asshole wakes up."

He outstretches his hand to reach for me, but I step back. He looks baffled by my resistance.

"How did you find me?" I repeat, squeezing the phone in one hand and my purse in the other.

A soft moan escapes Sean's mouth. His eyes open then close, then open again. They fix on me and he raises a hand.

Meanwhile, Joshua is staring at me in disbelief. He can tell I'm not going to budge until he gives me an answer, so he relents.

"I got a text, okay?" he says.

"From who?" I ask.

"I don't know. It was anonymous."

I wait for a follow-up that never comes. I suddenly feel the urge to be as far away from this man as possible because I see on his face the reason why I left him. I can see all the anger, frustration, impatience, and selfishness, just under the thin veil of fake heroism.

He's lying.

"You've been following me, haven't you?" I ask.

"What?" He lets out a chortle.

"The tracking app. You've been following me."

His mouth opens, but he doesn't deny it, and that's when I know I'm right. That text he'd sent me earlier only confirms it. He's been planning on getting to me, one way or another. It's too much of a coincidence for him to contact me tonight and then show up conveniently at Sean's place.

"Melissa, I..."

"Rachel told me someone else pinpointed my location with the tracking app. It was you, wasn't it? Do not lie to me."

"Okay, yes. I have used the tracking app to see where you are," he says. "But it was only because I was concerned for your safety."

I want to ask him how he did it, but I don't think I can stomach the details. Did he install the tracking app while I wasn't looking the last time we saw each other? Did he do it afterward?

Nope, I don't want to know.

"What exactly are you doing here?" I ask. "And tell me the truth."

"I told you. I got a text that you were in trouble, so I came to rescue you."

"Who sent you the text? And why would they do that?"

"I don't know."

"And then what happened—when you arrived?"

"Look, we can talk about this once we're out of here safely. Okay? Come on."

But I can't believe another word this man is saying.

"Melissa..." Sean's voice snaps my head to the kitchen.

The word sounds slurred. I can see him raising his head and hand. He says another word I don't understand immediately, but then my brain registers it, like a slow-loading internet image.

"Run."

Joshua takes a fervent step toward me and grabs me forcibly by the hand. I drop my phone, but that's okay. My hand is already inside my purse, and I'm pulling out the pepper spray that Rachel had given me before I left the apartment.

I point the object at Joshua's face and squeeze the top. The thing hisses as a spray of brown flies toward Joshua's face. His eyes are squeezed shut, and he's screaming. His grip on my wrist releases instantly, but I don't stop pepper-spraying him even when he's on the floor.

He's on his back, his hands held over his eyes, and he's screaming in pain. By then, Sean gets up. He stumbles toward me, and I'm about to spray him, too, but then I see that his intention isn't malicious.

"Are you okay?" he asks.

"What happened?"

"When you went to get the wine, he broke inside. I remember him grabbing a bottle, and then everything else is a blur."

"You're not the one who locked me in the cellar?"

Sean looks visibly perplexed. "What? No, of course not. Why would I do something like that? I told you. He broke inside and knocked me out."

"Then it must have been him." I point to Joshua.

He's still writhing on the floor. He'll continue to do so for the next hour or two. I have never been pepper-sprayed before, but I heard it burns like hell.

I don't feel sorry for Joshua, though. He deserves it. And after this, I'm hoping he'll finally be locked away for a long time.

"Who is this guy anyway? You sound like you know him," Sean says.

"He's um..." I gulp. "He's my ex."

"No way."

"Yes."

"I didn't realize you dated burglars."

"Me neither. But I guess I'm not surprised. He has a history of following me around, so I guess it was only a matter of time before something like this happened."

"Melissa, please... It's not like that. You have to believe me," Joshua hisses, but I'm not listening.

"We have to..." Sean starts and then grabs at his bleeding head and groans.

"You're hurt. We need to get you to a hospital," I say.

"I'm fine. It's you I'm worried about."

He's obviously not fine, but I can't help but appreciate the heroic gesture. I scoop my phone off the floor and dial 911.

It isn't long before I see the flashing blue and red lights outside the window.

Part 2

Chapter 13

I don't know where the time flies. After the police arrive, everything sort of melds together. I vaguely remember talking with the police officers and going with Sean to the hospital so they could take a look at his head.

"Don't worry, I'll be fine," he tells me before they rush him inside the doctor's office.

I don't see him after that. It may sound selfish, but I don't have enough room in my head after that for him. All I keep thinking about is Joshua breaking in and ruining my date with Sean. I don't think I'll ever be able to look at Sean the same way anyway.

Not after that night.

Any chances we had of a successful relationship were snuffed out by Joshua. In a way, he's won. He's in custody, awaiting trial, but no matter what happens, no matter how many years he gets, he will have left his mark on me.

Sometimes, I think that's exactly what he wanted all along. If he can't have me, then he might as well traumatize me so much that I never look at another man the same way.

I know I'm exaggerating. I'll get better someday. Right now, I just need time for that. And when I do get better, I'm going to start dating so hard that I'll meet the man of my dreams and marry him and have a happy life...while Joshua rots in prison.

It will be my ultimate screw you to him.

But that day seems like an eternity away.

I've become too sensitive to the stimuli around me. Something as simple as the smell of wine or peanut butter, or the sound of the door slamming shut, can transport me back to that cellar. It only lasts for brief moments, but it's enough to disorient me.

I'm a lot more careful in the streets. If I feel like someone might be following me—and I get that feeling a lot these days just from seeing someone glancing in my direction—I move to a more crowded area. I also carry Rachel's pepper spray with me, and I'm thinking of getting a gun.

I know this all seems like too much for such a mild experience, but I can't express how vulnerable the entire event has left me feeling. Joshua had gone out of his way to locate me at the house of my date, knocked Sean out, locked me in the cellar, and then let me out, pretending to be the hero while blaming Sean as the perpetrator.

He won't admit to that, though. I'm told he's sticking with his story that he got an anonymous text about me being in danger and that, when he arrived, he got into a fight with Sean. According to his story, I was already in the cellar when he arrived.

Although the police weren't able to pinpoint which phone the anonymous text had come from, they speculate Joshua sent that text from a burner phone to himself to get the suspicion off of him.

The dealbreaker, however, is the fact that he'd been tracking me with the spy app. He swears it was for my safety, but the prosecutors don't see it that way.

Even if he did manage to convince me that Sean was the one who locked me down there, forensic evidence would have gotten to the bottom of the case. In today's age, it's pretty much impossible to completely scrub a crime scene.

It bothers me that Joshua refuses to admit to what he's done. I understand him. He wants to get off the hook, but the evidence is right there, in plain sight. Hell, if he pleads guilty, he'll get better time than by pleading not guilty, but he refuses to do so.

He's always been stubborn, but this is one situation where he won't be able to have his way just because he wants it.

I'm rambling.

Two weeks have passed, and life has resumed as normally as it can, given the circumstances. My parents flew out to see me for a few days after the incident, which has been really helpful emotionally. Then there's Rachel, to whom I owe my life.

What if I hadn't brought that pepper spray that night? How far would Joshua have gone to win me over? Things easily could have escalated, and either Sean or I could have gotten killed.

It's all in the past, I keep telling myself. Sometimes I believe it.

Really, for now, I'm just glad that I don't need to talk to the detectives anymore. I can't expect to start my healing process while I'm constantly forced to remember what happened that night.

But even though I can tell it's hindering my path to getting better, I can't help but feel a surge of joy whenever Sean texts me to see if I'm okay.

Chapter 14

"Hey," I tell Rachel as I step inside the apartment.

"Hi," she says.

I don't look directly at her, but I can see in my peripheral vision her head snapping at me. I don't need to see her face to understand she's giving me her trademark concerned look. She's gauging me to see whether I'm okay, whether something happened, or whether I'm going to have a panic attack out of nowhere.

I hate when she does that.

It makes me feel like a ticking bomb or a dangerous animal. No, it's less harmful but more annoying than that. I feel like she's looking at a baby and making sure it doesn't start crying at any moment.

Rachel is sitting on the couch, her hand stuck in a bag of chips while a TV show is playing in front of her. Being a programmer looks like so much fun. Not only do you get to work from home, but you also have the flexibility to arrange your working hours the way you want them.

But Rachel is under a lot more stress than me, that's a fact. Whenever I come back home and see the door to her room shut, it means she's focused on work. I hear the muffled clacking of the keyboard in there and, from time to time, a scream or a groan, indicating she has no idea how to debug something or whatever it is she's doing.

It's in those moments that I know it's best to make as little noise as possible. God forbid if I knock on her door or come in to ask her something. If she loses her focus, she gets really angry. Actually, in those moments, she's the one who's like a ticking bomb.

"How was your day?" Rachel asks.

"Good. Yours?" I ask as I drop my purse on the counter.

"Good. I'm still waiting for my manager to let me know whether that one client wants to go ahead with the project or not."

When Rachel is between projects, she pretty much does nothing on company time and still gets paid. Those are the times I envy her. But then there are times when I wake up in the middle of the night to grab a glass of water and I hear her typing away on her keyboard in her room, and I'm glad I'm not in her shoes.

"Hey, I was thinking," Rachel says. "There's this band coming to town this weekend. Wanna go see them?"

"I don't know, Rach. I kinda wanted to sit home and have a lazy weekend."

"Oh, come on. It's been a while since we went out anywhere."

"I know." I plop onto the couch next to her. "I really just want to have some time to do stuff on my own, you know?"

"Yeah, I get it."

I like how she's understanding. Rachel is never the kind of person who's going to push me to go somewhere or do something, even if she knows pushing me would be good for me. If I say no, she's respectful.

"Well, if you change your mind, I'm down to go. We don't even need tickets. I know a guy who can get us in," Rachel says.

"Do we need to flash him or something for it?" I ask.

"What? No. Darren would kill me if I did something like that. His jealousy can be irritating sometimes."

"I think it's cute. I wish I had a guy who would get jealous enough to forbid me from flashing other people."

Just then, I feel a buzz in my pocket. I pull out my phone and unlock it. It's a message from a person I hoped would grow tired of messaging me and disappear.

Hey. Just wanted to check up on you and see how you were doing. I understand you probably don't want to hear from me again, but if you need anyone to talk to, I'm here.

"Well... maybe you do have a guy like that." Rachel carefully glances at me.

The worst thing about Sean's message is that it's so polite and sweet that I can't even be rude to him without feeling guilty.

I already spoke to Rachel about Sean and explained that I can't continue dating him because of what Joshua did. Too much happened that night for me to sweep it under the rug.

"Is it him?" Rachel asks, but I have a feeling she already knows.

"Yeah."

"What does he want?"

"He just says he's here if I need someone to talk to."

"See? I'm telling you, you're making a mistake ignoring him. Do you really want to let some douchebag like Joshua come between the two of you?"

"Well, no, but... I don't know. I just don't think I can look at him right now without remembering, you know?"

"Yeah, I understand. But I'm just saying..." Rachel says even before I begin to lay out the justifications. "You should at least talk to him. He obviously wants to see you."

"I know. I know." I don't know what else to say.

"You know, things must have been traumatizing for him, too. I mean, he's the one whose house got broken into, and he's the one who got knocked out by a bottle to the head."

I know she doesn't mean it like it sounds, but it sounds like she's trying to tell me to stop being so selfish.

And she's right.

During all this time, I haven't stopped to consider how Sean is feeling after all of this. I didn't even call to see how he was doing after he was taken to the hospital. For all I know, he might have suffered some serious consequences from the hit to the head. And then there's the fact that Rachel mentioned: His house got broken into.

Really, Sean has every right to hate me because Joshua is my ex, and he broke in and attacked us because of me. And yet, Sean is persistent. He messages me every couple of days, showing concern for my well-being.

I almost forgot he has a sister to take care of, and that makes me even more attracted to him because, despite everything that has happened and his caretaking responsibilities, he still finds the time to check up on me.

How can I be so selfish and not consider things from his angle?

"Look, the guy obviously likes you. A lot," Rachel says. "And he's worried about you. Do you know how rare that is these days? Back when I broke my leg while dating Matthew, he didn't even take a day off to come visit me in the hospital. And we had been dating for almost a year by then. Sean is a guy you went out with once, and look how caring he is."

"I thought you said there were lots of red flags with him." I grin.

Rachel shrugs. "I thought so, but I guess I was wrong. Whenever someone is really nice, I tend to think they're hiding something. But maybe I was wrong about Sean. Maybe he's just nice like that. I just can't help but think of that one guy from high school."

"Who?"

"The one who had a huge crush on you."

A lot of guys had a crush on me in high school—no, I'm not flexing—but I know immediately who Rachel is talking about.

"Steve? Scrawny Steve?" I ask.

"That's the one."

"Oh God."

I bite my lip. I didn't need that memory imposed on my brain right now. I still hate myself for being put in that situation.

Scrawny Steve was a kid who got bullied in high school all the time. I spoke to him a few times out of kindness, and I guess he took it as something more than that and showed up one day at my locker with a bouquet of roses, asking me to go out on a date with him.

It was the most embarrassing moment in high school for me. Everyone was staring at me, waiting for an answer. They even had their phones out to record videos of the whole thing. I still remember the cackling in the background and the pathetic look on Steve's face as he held out the flowers.

"I'm sorry, I have a boyfriend," I had told him, which was a lie.

Everyone knew that, too, but it was the only excuse I could think of at the time. I apologized one more time, but my words were drowned out by the howling of the guys close by. They didn't waste their time making fun of Steve.

Steve hung his head down and walked away while the other students made fun of him. He got bullied even harder after that, and I felt like it was my fault. One day, he dropped out of high school. We were told he had started going to a different school because of the extensive bullying.

"That guy was so freaking weird," Rachel says.

That he was. The cheerleaders in the locker room had caught him peeking at them twice, and he was sent to the principal's office for it. When the captain of the football team, who happened to be dating one of the cheerleaders, found out about it, he brought the entire team with him, and they beat Scrawny Steve up.

"Yeah." I nod.

I'm hoping that the topic about Scrawny Steve and Sean will be put to rest then, and it is, for a minute or so. Rachel and I watch TV in silence, and then she adds, "I'm just saying it might not be fair to you or to Sean. You should either tell him to leave you alone or go see him. That way you can finally conclude that topic."

"Yeah, you're right."

But as I stare down at my phone, I can't bring myself to do either. I want to type out a message to Sean, but whether I tell him to leave me alone or agree to see him, both feel like a commitment, and I don't think I can do that right now.

The right thing to do would be to stop being selfish and not leave Sean hanging, but whenever I start typing something to him, my thumb finds the backspace button and holds it until the message is gone.

The truth is I'm still drawn to Sean despite everything that happened that night. I keep thinking about our date and the amazing sex, and the way we stood in the kitchen, eating the sandwiches he made for us...

...and that's when things get ugly.

Damn you, Joshua. Why did you have to ruin the experience for me? Sean was the perfect man for me.

I hate Joshua so much that I wish I could go to prison and pepper-spray him again. In the moments when I feel really down, I remember how I incapacitated him that night.

It's not just the feeling of empowerment that I got from toppling a grown man. It's seeing him writhing on the floor and screaming in pain that brings me pleasure.

It may sound sadistic, but you have no idea the hell Joshua has put me through—I'm not talking just about what happened that night but throughout our relationship, too.

"I'm gonna go take a long bubble bath." I stand.

"Sure thing," Rachel says.

She's already focused on the TV screen again.

Even as I shut the bathroom door behind me and run the water in the tub, I can't help but glance at the phone, expecting the screen to light up with a message from Sean.

Chapter 15

Days continue to pass. It's around four weeks after the night of the incident, and I'm starting to feel like my life's getting back to normal.

It happened so gradually that I didn't realize it until I looked back and remembered how I felt the first week following Joshua's break-in. He's still awaiting trial, which is expected to be in about a month.

He wasn't granted bail in the meantime, much to my relief. I can't help but think that he would use his freedom to find me again, and I don't think things would end as well this time.

Sean has stopped messaging me. It's been a week, but I still jump to see if it's him whenever my phone buzzes with a useless notification from a social media app I haven't used in a while. I know I sound like a brat, but I miss getting messages from him.

I hadn't realized that him checking up on me gave me the slight boost I needed in my daily life. Just knowing I had someone who cared like that kept me going. Sure, I have my parents and Rachel, but being cared for by someone like Sean is in an entirely different category.

Anyway, it's my own fault.

I ignored him, and it was only natural that he would stop trying to contact me after a while. I regret it so much that I want to send him a message, but I once again feel like I'd be committing to something I can't keep my word for.

What if I message him, realize it was a mistake, and then ignore him? I would get his hopes up for nothing, and not to mention I'd give off the impression that I'm just looking for someone to boost my ego.

It's Saturday, and I have just finished my walk in the park and returned home. Rachel is there, sitting on the couch, and reading a book—lately, it feels as though she's grown roots onto that piece of furniture.

As soon as I walk in, her head snaps in my direction. Her eyes are wide, her face retaining a look of shock. I must be imagining things because the expression is gone just as fast, and she's focused on the book again.

"What took you so long?" she asks.

"The day's nice, so I sat at the park a little bit."

"Oh," Rachel says.

"What have you been up to?"

"Oh, nothing. Just the usual."

"Is that the same book?"

Rachel shifts in her seat. "What?"

"Is that the same book you've been reading this entire week?"

"Oh. Yes. It's a big one, and I'm not as fast a reader as I used to be."

She shifts again. That's when I start to notice something's wrong. Something is agitating her, but I don't know what.

"Rach? Is everything okay?" I ask.

She looks at me with a tight-lipped smile and gives me a series of nods. "Uh-huh."

That's how I know something is definitely up. Rachel is not a very subtle person. If something happens in her life that makes her distressed, I immediately notice it. If she's lying about something, I know it right away.

It's in the way her body language and the tone of her voice change. She becomes a little more erratic and fiddles with things, and her voice is higher-pitched.

I know right away that I won't be able to draw the information out of Rachel just by asking her what's up. This will take some chipping away.

I sit next to her and ask, "Want to tell me what's going on?"

Rachel's mouth pulls into a grimace, and she looks at me. She closes the book, and the corners of her eyebrows are arched upward. I was wrong. It looks like she's going to open up a lot easier than I expected.

"I'm sorry," she says.

"What are you sorry for?"

Just then, the doorbell rings.

I spin to look at the door as if it will let me see through it, then back at Rachel. Rachel has a guilty look on her face.

"Don't hate me," she says.

"What did you do?" I ask.

Rachel puts the book next to her on the couch and stands up.

"Rach, please tell me that's the food you ordered," I say.

"I'm sorry. I know I shouldn't have, but I contacted Sean."

"You *what?!*"

Now I'm standing, too. My heart is racing. I wait for Rachel to tell me she's joking, but the punchline never comes.

"I messaged him from my phone and told him to come here. I knew it was the only way to get you to talk to him," she says.

"Rachel!"

The doorbell rings again. Sean knows we're inside. He's not going to leave now. Unlike texting, I can't ignore him in real life. Not when he's standing outside my apartment door.

I start to get angry. Rachel went behind my back to contact Sean and arrange a meeting with him even though I didn't agree to it. How can I trust my roommate if she's going to pull off something like this?

"I'm not going to talk to him. Rachel, I'm serious. I'm going to lock myself in my room, and when I come out, I want him gone. Do you understand?"

Rachel defensively raises her hands. "Look, I know you like him, and I think if you just talk to him, you'll see that you guys can work it out because you're stronger than Joshua. Please, Melissa."

"I can't believe you would do this to me, Rachel," I say, offended.

The doorbell rings again. The air in the room feels heavy. Rachel walks around the couch and strides toward the door.

"Rachel, stop!" I call out.

"Just give him five minutes. Talk to him for five minutes, and if you're not feeling it, we'll tell him to leave. I'm sure he's going to be respectful."

It's not like I have a choice at this point. Sean is already at the door. I could insist that Rachel tell him to go away, but I think she's right. This is my chance to put an end to this chapter. Sean and I are going to talk things out like real adults and then go our own separate ways.

"Five minutes. And then I'm done," I say.

"I promise." Rachel smiles.

She reaches for the door. I cross my arms and look away although I don't know why exactly.

"Hi, Sean," Rachel says.

"Hi there. Pleasure to meet you," Sean says.

Hearing his voice instantly transports me back to the night we spent together, but strangely, I don't remember the bad things. Only the good ones.

I sneak a glance at the door to see Sean smiling widely as he and Rachel shake hands. I vaguely realize that this is the first time they meet in person.

"Come on in," Rachel says.

Sean thanks her and steps inside. Our eyes meet, and I feel the urge to look away.

"Hi," I say.

"Hi," he says back.

We stand in silence, staring at each other for a protracted moment. I glance at Rachel, silently asking what the heck we're supposed to do now. She misreads my gaze because she says, "I just remembered that I have an errand to run downtown. I'll leave you two alone so you can talk."

I clench my jaw, shooting daggers at her with my eyes, silently trying to tell her not to dare leave me alone here with Sean.

She grabs her coat, steps outside, and, while holding onto the doorknob, says, "I'll be back in five minutes."

She winks at me and closes the door behind her.

At least I know she'll honor her promise of not making me talk to Sean for more than five minutes.

Chapter 16

For a while, awkward silence lingers between me and Sean. I try hard to think of something to say, but no words come to my mind. The visit is unexpected, and if I at least knew he'd be coming, I'd have taken the time to prepare for it.

"Nice place you got here," he says.

"It's okay." I shrug. "It's not a mansion like yours."

He laughs. "Well, I like cozy places."

I realize he's still standing at the entrance with his hands in his pockets, so I offer him to sit. He thanks me and sits on the couch.

"Sorry, it's a little messy in here," I say, moving Rachel's blanket and book out of the way and taking a seat next to him. "I'm sorry, would you like something to drink?"

"No, I'm good. Thank you, though."

More silence. What a productive way to spend five minutes. Why am I so stumped with words all of a sudden?

"So..." he starts.

I'm hoping there's a continuation of that sentence, but it doesn't happen. He's just glancing around the apartment, seemingly admiring the décor.

"So, how's Anna? This must have been really stressful for her," I ask.

"I didn't tell her anything," Sean says. "I didn't want to worry her. It's not healthy to break big, terrible news to people with such conditions. But she's doing okay."

"I'm happy to hear that. How's your head?" I ask, suddenly remembering that he got whacked with a bottle by Joshua.

"Oh, my head. It's fine. The doctors say I suffered a mild concussion, but it's no big deal."

I feel guilty for not checking up on him.

"Forget about it. It's you I'm worried about," Sean says.

"Me? I'm not the one who got knocked unconscious," I say.

"Yeah, but that was just physical pain. You're the one who got off worse."

I know what he means, so I look down and nod.

"I was really worried about you, Melissa," he says. "I know how traumatic the entire experience must have been. It's the reason why I wanted to give you some space, but I couldn't resist messaging you. I'm sorry if this is too direct, but... I missed you."

I missed you, too, I want to say but keep the thoughts to myself.

I bring myself to look at him. He's staring at me, and I once again remember that night we spent together. I want to kiss him. No, not want. *Need.* I feel like his touch is going to dispel all the bad from me.

But I don't do anything. I'm still not one hundred percent sure if that's what he wants, too. He looks like it, but I've been known to misinterpret the signs in the past.

"Melissa." Sean's hand drifts toward me.

His fingers touch mine. I feel a warmth slithering up my hand all the way to my chest.

"I feel like we have a special connection," Sean says. "I've never felt about anyone the way I feel about you. The girls I went out on a date with... I usually forget about them after a day or two. But you... I can't seem to get you out of my head."

The feeling is mutual. I find myself thinking about him a lot. It's usually during the quiet moments like between classes—or when I'm back from work and watching TV or browsing social media.

Sometimes, though, he slinks into my mind even when I'm busy. I'll be teaching a classroom full of children how to spell certain words, and all of a sudden, the inappropriate image of me and Sean rolling in his bed enters my mind.

All those thoughts, however, are tainted by my time in the cellar and Joshua's untimely appearance. But right now, I can't remember Joshua. I can't remember the cellar. I don't see anything or anyone except Sean, and it feels like I'm being pulled toward him by a powerful magnet.

I don't offer any resistance. Our lips meet, and I am once again overcome by that same electrical pleasure that I felt on our date. While exploring each other's mouths, I ask myself why I resisted this in the first place.

Rachel had been right to invite Sean here, and I'll have to thank her for it later. I'll hate watching her gloat with her "told you so" attitude, but I don't care. Right now, I only care that Sean and I are kissing.

The world feels right once again.

That bliss is interrupted by the sound of the door opening. Sean and I stop kissing and turn around to see Rachel standing at the door. She's earlier than I expected. It couldn't have been more than a few minutes, and I wonder if she's just been standing in front of the door, waiting for the time to pass.

For once, I wish she would have broken her promise.

"Oh, I'm sorry. I didn't realize..." She stumbles over her words. "I'm just going to... Actually, I just remembered that I have something more important to take care of. I'm just going to grab my things. Don't mind me."

She flashes me a double thumbs up before disappearing inside her room. Sean can't see her from this angle.

"Okay, just looking for my phone! Oh, and gotta grab my wallet! Now, where did I put it?" Rachel is talking from the other room.

Meanwhile, Sean and I are staring and smiling at each other.

"I know this is sudden, but how much time do you have right now?" I ask him.

"For you? As much as I want. What did you have in mind?"

"How about we go back to your place? We'll have a lot more privacy there."

His smile widens. "Really? Wait, you're not bothered by... well, you know?"

I shake my head. "I figure the best thing I can do is face my demons. The sooner I start, the sooner I can beat them."

"Sounds good."

"But... I don't want you to get the wrong idea. I want to take things slow."

"I'm a patient man. You're worth it." He brushes my hair behind my ear.

He stands and takes my hand. Rachel emerges from the room, still talking about the things she needs to find before leaving.

"Rachel, it's fine. You can stay. Sean and I are going back to his place," I say.

"Oh," Rachel says.

She sounds surprised, but not in a bad way.

"Are you sure?" she asks.

"Yes."

She has the same concerned look on her face as Sean did just moments ago.

"I'll be back later," I tell Rachel, and then Sean and I are out of the apartment and running toward the elevator, and we're kissing while it descends.

Fifteen minutes later, when he pulls his car up in front of his house, he kills the engine, and we sit in silence for a moment. He looks at me and asks, "Are you sure about this? I can get us a hotel if you like."

"I'm sure." I nod. "But I'm not going anywhere near the cellar."

"Don't worry," Sean says. "I already closed it off. It doesn't exist anymore."

Chapter 17

Although Sean and I don't officially admit we're dating, that's how things are.

What else do you call it when you spend every day together kissing, making love, and holding hands while walking? We're certainly more than friends, but we're taking it slow, as per my request.

I'm fine with that. I'm just enjoying getting to know him. I know this won't last forever—either Sean or I will want to move things to the next level—but I'm done worrying about the future. Thinking about what might happen ahead has brought me nothing but anxiety.

I don't have a problem with Sean's house anymore. I admit that I was a little skeptical that day when Rachel invited him over, but one step inside showed me that I was afraid of the idea of the house rather than the house itself.

We give power to things that make us feel weak. I was determined to regain control, and what better place to start than the one where the incident happened in the first place?

Sean hadn't lied. The door to the cellar was no longer where it stood. A wall was in its place, perfectly blended with the rest of the house. Someone who hadn't seen the cellar wouldn't look at that wall twice.

But I did.

I could see through that wall. I could see the dark staircase leading down into the brightly illuminated room. I could see the wine holders and the bottles inside them. I could see the glass cabinet with the wine at the end of the room. I could see shards of glass and spilled wine from how I broke the bottle in an attempt to defend myself.

I swear I could smell the winey air and feel the freezing temperature of the room just by staring at that wall, but just as quickly as those thoughts arrived, they left my mind.

"You're not going to have anything else instead of the cellar there?" I'd asked Sean.

"No." He shook his head. "I can't. Whenever I looked at it, I remembered you being trapped in there. The thought of you being stuck there, banging on the door, scared to death, drove me insane. I had to get rid of it."

"Thank you," I'd said.

And I meant it. I'm so glad he got rid of that room. I honestly hate anything that's built under the ground—basements, cellars, garages, storm shelters...

I know they serve their purpose, but I just hate being under tons and tons of concrete, away from the sun.

I've also asked him to move that expensive vase from his bedroom because I almost knock it down every time we go there, but he says he really likes the way it looks on the nightstand. It's his house after all, so I can't complain. I just can't help but think that one of these days it'll end up on the floor and shattered into a million pieces.

With my new boyfriend in my life, I hardly ever think about Joshua. Until, one day, when I get a call from an unknown number while Sean and I are watching a movie at his place.

I usually don't answer unknown numbers anymore. It's either reporters asking to interview me or spam calls. But it had been a while since I got one, and something tells me this might be important.

"Excuse me. I think I need to take this," I say as I stand up and leave the living room.

I enter the library and swipe the green button to answer the call. "Hello?"

"Hello? Is this you, Melissa?" a masculine voice on the other end asks.

Oh no. Oh no. Oh no.

I recognize that voice. It's a voice I hoped to never again hear in my life.

For a moment, I consider hanging up and turning off my phone. But I can't bring myself to do it. No matter what happened, I still have deep respect for Joshua's dad.

"Who's asking?" I pretend not to know who it is, but I'm just trying to buy myself time.

"It's Howard," he says. "Please, I'm begging you, don't hang up on me."

I'm about to tell him that I have to go, but I'm compelled to listen to what he has to say. Howard has always shown nothing but respect for me, and I could sense how dear I was to him. The feeling was mutual, and that's what made the break-up all the more difficult.

"I can't talk to you, Mr. Dawson," I say.

"I know. I've been advised to not contact you because it can only bring more harm. Josh wanted to talk to you, too, but they won't let him. I think it's a good thing, but I, as a parent, have to talk to you to make things right."

I remain silent because I sense he's about to say something.

"Melissa, my son is innocent," he exclaims.

Something tells me he's been rehearsing the speech but that this is not the way it was supposed to go down. Emotions are controlling him, which I can hear from the tone of his voice.

"Mr. Dawson..." I say, but I can't figure out what to say next.

Of course he's going to think Joshua is innocent. He's his dad. Every parent wants to see the best in their child, even if they're a monster.

"Please, just hear me out," he says, and his voice is trembling, sounding like it's on the verge of tears. "I know my son. He's not a saint, but he would never do anything like this. He swears he would never hurt you."

I can't listen to this anymore. Howard Dawson is clearly in denial. I realize I've been more than fair by giving him a chance to speak up, but he has nothing of value to add, nothing new that would make me change my mind about Joshua.

"I have to go, Mr. Dawson," I say.

"Please, wait! If he gets convicted, he's going to face up to forty years in prison. Please, don't ruin his life like this. Please."

I'm the one ruining his life? That sentence makes me boil with anger.

"I have to go," I say. "I wish you all the best, Mr. Dawson."

I hang up against his begging and crying. I stare down at the phone, expecting it to start ringing again. I don't realize how badly my hands are shaking until then.

"Hey," I hear a voice at the door.

I turn to see Sean peeking inside.

"Everything okay?" he asks.

I hope he can't see how distressed I am.

"Yeah," I say, but I sound out of breath even to myself.

"Who was that?" he asks.

"Oh, um..." I look down at the phone. "Wrong number."

Sean steps inside the library and approaches me. He caresses my cheek, and I instantly feel relief flooding my body.

"Hey, are you sure you're okay?" he asks me.

"Yeah." I nod.

And I am.

"Cool. Wanna get back to the movie, then?" he asks.

"I would love to," I say.

He turns to leave, but I stop him. I give him a long kiss.

"What was that for?" He looks surprised.

I shrug. "Can't a girl express her gratitude for having such a perfect boyfriend?"

He seems content with that response. We go back to the living room, and I don't think about the call again that night.

It's all thanks to Sean.

Whenever he's close to me, I feel like nothing bad can happen.

Chapter 18

In the following days, my phone rings a few more times. It's an unknown number again, and I don't answer it this time. I go through my call history, and I realize that it's not Joshua's dad.

It's someone else, but I don't care. Nothing good can come from answering an unknown number.

Besides, if it's an emergency, they'll send a message to tell me to pick up.

I try to focus all my attention on Sean, but what Joshua did sometimes distracts me, and I hate him for it. Rachel tells me that I shouldn't harbor any emotions toward him, especially not hate, because I'm just giving him more power than he has—and he has none.

I can't help it, though. Even though Sean and I have agreed to take things slow, I sometimes feel like we're rushing things too much. None of this would have happened if only I refused to come to his place on the first date.

Now, we're already saying I love you to each other, and we're practically inseparable outside of work. Even Rachel complained that I spend way too much time with him and that it's been a while since she and I had a girls' night out.

She's right, and I need to be a better friend. I can't throw her aside just because I have a boyfriend, no matter how obsessed I am with him. That's why I promised Rachel we'd go and do this weekend whatever she wants.

I'm already dreading it because I just know the activity Rachel will organize for us will involve staying up past midnight and being in a loud, crowded place. But she's my friend, and that's what friends do—they do things they hate because they know it will make the other person happy.

On a Thursday afternoon, I come back from work, take a shower, and get ready to meet Sean at his place. He's working late today, so I'm going to take an Uber there instead.

"You're going to Sean's again?" Rachel asks.

"Yeah." I nod when I walk out of the bathroom.

"Okay," Rachel theatrically exclaims from the couch.

She has her laptop in her lap. Lately, she's taken to working in the living room. I guess she needed a change of scenery in order to stay motivated.

She's tapping her nails on the side of her laptop rhythmically, a pensive look on her face.

"All right, I can see you want to say something, so say it," I say.

She looks at me. "Just... don't rush things with Sean too much, okay?"

"Red flags again?" I ask.

She doesn't respond.

"Not this again. We've been through this already," I say.

"I know, but I just can't help but be worried. You said he's super rich and has a huge house, right?"

"Yeah, he works for the biggest consulting company in the city."

"They pay so well? If I'd known, I never would have become a programmer. I really wish I could see that big library you mentioned, though."

"I'd love to show you, but..."

"I know. He's a private person."

Some silence lingers between us, and I can sense Rachel is still skeptical.

"Look, he hasn't done anything yet to show me he's a psycho or a weirdo, right?" I ask.

"Yeah." Rachel nods.

"Then you're probably imagining things."

"I guess."

"There. Mystery solved, then. And can we please not talk about this again? You're making me paranoid, for Christ's sake."

"You *should* be paranoid. It's the only way you'll ever be safe."

I sigh again, silently disagreeing with her statement. If I say it aloud, she'll find ways to argue why I'm wrong. But I'm not. I don't want to live my life pretending I'm navigating a minefield.

"I'm going out. I'll be back in a few hours," I say.

"Say hi to Sean," Rachel says.

She doesn't even need to ask where I'm going anymore. I can sense a hint of passive aggression in her voice, but I ignore it and let her continue working.

For once, I've found a man who makes me happy, and I intend to fully surrender myself to him and let him take the reins.

CHAPTER 19

When I arrive, Sean is inside the living room with his phone pressed up against his ear. He's saying something to the person on the other end—some business mumbo-jumbo that I don't understand.

That mysteriousness and his assertiveness make him so sexy. I'm tempted to be naughty with him while he's on the call, but it's a domain I don't know if he'd be comfortable in, so I decide it's best to communicate about it first.

"Okay, let me know. Bye," Sean says as he hangs up.

He turns his attention to me and smiles. "Sorry about that."

He approaches, gives me a kiss, then strides into the kitchen, "Want something to drink?"

"I'm good," I say.

"Okay. Well, make yourself at home. It's not like you're a guest here anymore anyway."

Is he implying what I think he is? We haven't been dating for long, but I have to admit I haven't considered moving in together just yet. Sure, I spend more nights here than I do at home, but it's non-committal. I can grab my things and leave whenever I want.

If I move in, though, that's going to be a lot more difficult. I'm as excited as I'm terrified.

"You don't mind if I have one, do you? It's been a long day," Sean says, holding a bottle of gin.

"Not at all," I say, both glad and disappointed that the topic of moving in has reached a dead end.

For now.

"Thanks," he says.

He's placed his phone on the counter and is pouring the alcohol into a glass. It looks like he's pouring more than usual, so I assume he must have had a stressful day.

This is only confirmed when his phone starts buzzing on the counter. Sean groans, runs a hand down his face, then slides the phone closer to him. He stares at the screen for a moment then taps on it to decline the call.

"Work?" I ask.

"Yeah. They can be pretty incompetent sometimes," he says while typing out a message to the person who just tried to call him, I'm assuming.

"If it's a bad moment, I can come back some other time," I suggest.

"No! Not at all." He shakes his head. "Sorry, let me just send this message, and then I'm all yours."

I smile and nod as I make my way to the couch. Sean joins me shortly after. He places his drink on the coffee table then leans in to kiss me. I love it when he focuses all his attention on me like this. Even after almost two months of dating, I still don't get sick of it.

He makes me feel pretty and valuable and like I'm worth everything in this world. It's something Joshua should have done for me, but he never did. His loss. I look back at everything that has happened, and I realize that I wouldn't change a thing because it has inevitably led to Sean and me falling in love.

"Listen, I still haven't taken a shower," Sean says. "It's been kind of busy after work with calls and all that. Can you give me ten minutes?"

"Take as long as you need," I say.

He kisses me, takes a sip of his drink, then stands up.

"You can join me if you like," he says.

"Hm." I tap a finger on my chin. "I might surprise you. I might not. I guess you'll have to wait and find out."

He smiles then starts toward the stairs. "Feel free to watch TV or grab something to eat or drink while I'm gone."

"Okay!"

I'm left in silence. I pull my phone out of my purse and, like I always do, I scroll social media. I'm really considering deleting my social media apps. It's not like I need them for anything except to feel connected to the world, and I spend way too much time on them.

Sure, they're okay when I'm waiting in line for something or whatever, but these things were created to keep us addicted.

Loud buzzing snaps my head up from the screen of my phone. I look toward the counter to see Sean's phone still there. Someone from work must be calling him. I ignore the buzzing until it stops.

I consider going upstairs to tell Sean someone called him, but Sean values his private time. He always says that, if it's an emergency outside his working hours, they should call 911. I like that attitude. His performance shows how much of a dedicated employee he is, but it also sends the message that he will not sacrifice his free time for the company.

Not even twenty seconds later, his phone starts ringing again. I try to ignore it once more, but that's when I realize that maybe it really is an emergency and that I should tell Sean. I know if I received two consecutive missed calls in a row, I'd call back to see what the fuss was all about.

By the time I decide whether I should go upstairs and tell Sean about it or not, the ringing has already stopped again. I continue scrolling social media on my phone, but then the buzzing starts once more.

Now I know for sure that it's an emergency.

I stand up, put my phone into my pocket, and stride over to the counter. I know I shouldn't, but I reach over and pick it up. I intend to tell the person on the other end that Sean will call them back. I just hope Sean won't get upset with me for doing so.

By then, the phone stops ringing.

"Darn," I say.

I swipe to unlock the screen and realize that all three missed calls had come from Anna.

Sean's sister.

I freeze. Three missed calls in just a few minutes. I feel like I should tell Sean about this immediately. It's gotta be an emergency if she's calling like that. Maybe she's having an episode or has been in an accident.

I hold on to the phone in hopes of receiving a fourth call from her so I can answer it.

It would be the first time I'd talk to her. Not a great way to meet.

The wallpaper on Sean's screen catches my attention. It's a picture of me sleeping in his bed. I'm without makeup, my hair is bedraggled, and I'm covered up to my chest. I look terrible, but Sean must have liked seeing me in that state since he snapped the photo and put it on his wallpaper.

I'm honored, but I do wish he would have put a more flattering picture of me there. I wonder what other pictures he's taken of me while I wasn't looking. I enter his gallery and stare at the bevy of albums in there.

One in particular catches my eye. An album titled "Melissa." I can see in the album's thumbnail the two of us posing for a selfie, and my heart lights up with warmth. I smile as I open the album and tap on the picture.

I linger on each picture for a few seconds, remembering the moment it was taken. I feel the surge of emotions from the pictures rushing into me as if I'm transported right back there to the moment they were taken.

I see a few pictures of me sleeping, and I buzz past those. I can see he's taken a lot more pictures of me unaware than I realized. I'm staring at the camera, though, and it's mostly candid moments like me standing in front of the counter with a sandwich in my hand and my mouth full, or getting dressed and giving him a look, or glancing in his direction from the park bench.

I remember there were a few times when I asked him if he was taking pictures of me, and he said no. What a liar.

This man adores me. I don't see why he does, but it's like that, and it makes me love him even more. I suddenly get the urge to join Sean in the shower and show him how much I love him.

That is until I get to the next picture. When I do, I can feel the smile on my face physically getting wiped. The warmth is replaced by a plunge of iciness, and I feel as though a freight train has just hit me.

It's a picture of me getting out of work, taken from a distance. I'm staring somewhere to the left, unaware of the person taking the picture. I stare at the photo then zoom in. I try to consider when this was taken, but I can't reach a conclusion.

Something inside me tells me not to swipe to the next picture, but I do it anyway.

This one is of me taking a walk in the park. I remember this. It was just a few weeks ago. I had sat down because the day was nice. Nobody was at the park at that time. Nobody that I saw anyway. Just like the previous picture, this one was taken from a distance.

The next picture shows me standing in front of the *Picnic Place* restaurant. It's from the night Sean and I went out on our first date. In the picture, I'm standing with the purse in my hands, staring off to the side, waiting for him to show up.

The next few pictures are similar. Me standing in front of the restaurant, only I'm looking elsewhere. In one of the pictures, it looks as though my eyes have met with the camera. I must have looked straight at it and not seen it.

My hands are trembling. And yet, I can't stop myself from swiping to the next picture. Each one gets progressively worse.

I see pictures of me leaving my building to go to work, stopping at Starbucks for coffee, sitting with Joshua in a café... I see a picture taken from a window of me and Joshua naked in bed from back when we were still dating.

I exit the full screen and scroll to the bottom of the album. There are hundreds and hundreds of pictures of me taken long before Sean and I even met.

If you stare at anything long enough, it opens up to you and tells you its story.

I remember the girls whose pictures I saw on the camera. I feel like throwing up. I'm glad I had a small meal. Otherwise, my puke would have been all over the kitchen.

Still, I hold a hand over my mouth to stop myself from gagging. Tears blur my vision. My knees quaver with weakness, barely able to hold the weight of my body.

Then, the phone starts ringing again. It's Anna. I don't think. I just tap on the green button to accept the call. I raise the phone to my ear and wait. An alarmingly long moment of silence passes, but I think I detect breathing on the other side.

"Sean? Oh, thank God. I've been worried about you," a distressed, feminine voice says.

"Hello. Um, this is Sean's girlfriend, Melissa. Sean is in the shower right now," I recite.

There's a pause.

"Girlfriend?" she asks.

"Yes. My name's Melissa."

"Melissa?" Anna asks.

I feel as though I'm speaking to someone who doesn't understand English. I'm about to tell her I'll get Sean, but then Anna speaks up again.

"Where's Sean?" she asks.

"He's in the shower," I repeat.

I can tell something's wrong with Anna. She sounds anxious or panicked. I need to tell Sean.

"Hold on, I'm going to get Sean right away," I say.

"Wait! No!" Anna screeches into the phone, hurting my eardrum. "Don't tell him I called. Please."

"Why?"

More silence until Anna breaks it. "Has he... told you anything?"

"About what?"

"About..." Her sentence trails.

About what? Anna's schizophrenia?

"Can you please just tell me if he's taking his medication regularly?" Anna asks.

"What?" I ask.

My head is spinning. I'm not even sure I heard her right.

"His schizophrenia medication. Please tell me he's taking it regularly."

I remain silent, too dumbstruck to respond to that.

"Hello? Are you still there?" she asks.

"Yes. Yes, I am."

"Well then, is he taking his meds or not?"

"Um... I don't... I don't think so. I mean, he's never told me anything about it, and I've never seen him take anything."

"Dammit!" Another shout that makes my ear hurt. "I keep telling him he can't stop taking the meds just because he feels better. I'll have to tell the doctor about this. Please, don't let Sean know I told you anything."

I can sense the conversation is about to end, so I intervene. "Wait a second. I have so many questions. What meds? What's going on?"

"He hasn't told you anything, has he?"

"About what?" I want to scream into the phone because Anna is so cryptic.

I hear a sigh on the other side. Then Anna says, "Sean has schizophrenia. He has to regularly take his medication, or he starts to... get bad."

"Wait, he told me *you* have schizophrenia."

Anna goes silent again. "Melissa, right? Sean is not being honest with you."

"Yes, I can tell, but—"

"You don't know the half of it. Please, I suggest you get out of there and never speak to Sean again."

"Well, wait—"

But Anna has already hung up. I stare at the screen, wondering if the conversation actually happened or if I imagined the whole thing.

The nausea that had seized my gut is now even stronger. The conversation with Anna replays in my mind over and over. I see the images taken without my consent flashing before my eyes. I hear Anna's panicked voice asking me if Sean is taking his medicine.

I enter the messaging history with Anna from Sean's phone and read some of the final messages.

Please, just pick up your phone, Sean, Anna's message says.

You have to tell her the truth, another one says.

No. She wouldn't understand. She'd hate me if she knew the truth, Sean's reply says.

Who's she? Are they talking about me? And what truth? The fact that he's the one with schizophrenia, and not his sister?

There are more messages from Anna, all of them asking Sean if he's taking his medication and if she can come for a visit. He rarely responds.

The buzzing in my pocket makes me jump. I exit the messages, lock Sean's phone, and place it on the counter where I found it, then I fish my own phone out. Rachel is calling me.

I raise the phone to my ear. "Hello?"

"Melissa, where are you?" Rachel asks.

I can hear agitation in her voice.

"I'm at Sean's place," I say.

"Can he hear me?"

"No. He's in the shower."

"Okay, good. Listen to me very carefully. You need to get out of there right now."

"What? What's going on?" My voice is shaky, and Rachel's tone of urgency doesn't make me feel any more composed.

"Don't freak out, okay? I had a bad feeling about Sean, so I looked him up online."

"Okay, and?"

I don't know if I can stomach the details right now, but I have to know. I have to hear the truth so I can decide how bad it really is.

"You said he works for a big consulting company, right?"

"Yes."

"Well, I couldn't find any information online about it, which is weird. So, I called the company and asked about Sean, and they claim they don't have anyone under that name working there."

My stomach is twisting into knots. I need to sit because my knees might collapse under my weight any moment now. But I can't move. My feet are rooted to the floor. My ear hurts because I'm pressing the phone so hard against it.

Oh God. Anna wasn't lying. He's crazy, and he's been following me for a while now. He's had an unhealthy crush on me this entire time. Has he been biding his time, waiting for the right moment to meet with me?

You don't know the half of it, Anna's words echo in my mind.

"Melissa, I have a really bad feeling about this. He hid the truth from you. That's not even a red flag anymore. It's a frigging flag on fire. Please, just take this moment while he's in the shower to get out of there."

"Sorry I took so long," a voice in the room says.

It's Sean, and he's right behind me.

Chapter 20

It takes everything in me not to whirl around.

"Is that him? It's him, isn't it?" Rachel asks.

Slowly, I turn around and force a smile. Sean's staring at me. He's wearing a sleeveless shirt and boxers.

"Rach, I'm going to have to call you back," I say in a voice as neutral as possible.

"No, wait!"

But before Rachel can say anything more, I hang up and slide the phone into my pocket.

"Was that your roommate?" he asks.

"Yeah." I nod.

"What did she want?"

"She, uh, was just curious when I was coming back home," I blurt.

The way he's staring at me makes me think he doesn't believe me.

"Already? But you just left," he says as he strides over to me.

I once again have to fight the urge to wince or recoil. I can't let him know I figured out what's up. I have to play it cool until I'm out of his house.

I know what to do. I'll just make a vague excuse about not feeling too well. But I can't do it right away. It'll be suspicious. I should wait a little bit. At least ten minutes or so.

The question is: Will I be able to pretend for that long? Will he see through me and notice the fear? I sometimes feel like he's able to read my mind, and I've never had a problem with that.

Until now.

Now I can't stand his gaze because it makes me feel like he's scrambling my brain with a fork.

"Yeah, she's bored, I guess. Working from home can do that," I say and feign a chuckle.

Sean's eyes drift to his phone on the counter then back at me. He approaches me, plants a kiss on my lips, and I hope to God he doesn't notice how stiff I am from being touched by him.

The kiss quickly ends, and Sean grabs his phone off the counter and unlocks it. He stares at the screen with a reticent look. I observe him, trying to gauge whether he's suspecting anything. The moment seems to last forever.

"Did anybody call while I was gone?" he asks.

What should I say? Do I tell him the truth? Do I lie and say I haven't heard anything? He won't see the missed calls on his screen. Only when he enters the call history with Anna will he understand that there's a call he somehow missed.

And that's when he might start to suspect me.

"Yeah, your phone actually rang a few times while you were gone," I say.

I don't know if that's the right thing to say, but I don't have enough time to consider my answer, so I just blurt out the one that seems more right.

"I, uh, tried to answer it to tell them you're in the shower, but it stopped ringing by the time I picked up," I add quickly.

Please don't suspect anything.

"Okay," he says, his eyes momentarily flitting in my direction then back at the screen.

"Was it work?" I ask.

"Yeah," he lies as he locks the phone and puts it back on the counter.

"Aren't you going to call them back?"

"No, it's not important. They can wait." Sean smiles.

"I think you should call them. It sounds like they might need your help."

"That's their problem. I'm not working right now, so they can handle things on their own."

This interaction has at least proven one thing to me—Sean is a liar.

He must have seen that Anna was the one who called him, and yet he blatantly lied by telling me it was work. I don't try to find a rationalization for it anymore. He lied. I don't need to know the reason for it.

"So, what do you want to do today? There's a fair in town. Want to go check it out?"

"Um..." I consider that for a moment. "Actually, I kind of feel sick all of a sudden."

"Oh no. Are you coming down with something?" he asks with concern in his voice, but it sounds disingenuous.

I hadn't intended on making the excuse so soon, but I can't help it. The panic that overwhelms me feels like it's going to make me explode. I need to get away from Sean as soon as possible.

When our eyes meet, I don't see Sean anymore. I don't see Joshua, either. I see someone far more terrifying that's been hidden from me this entire time.

How haven't I noticed it before?

"I'm not sure. I just feel like I need to lie down," I say.

"If you want to get some rest, you can take my bed upstairs. I'll take good care of you," Sean says.

It would have sounded heavenly five minutes ago. Now, staying in this house another minute is an absolute nightmare.

"Thanks, but I'd better get home. I don't want you to contract whatever I have," I say.

"Okay, let me give you a ride then."

I'm just glad he's not trying to convince me to stay. Even though I'd much rather use an Uber to get home, I don't want to be too suspicious, so I agree to let him take me home.

It doesn't matter anyway. Once we're outside this house, I'll be safe. In the worst-case scenario, I can barge out the door and call for help or at least roll down the window and scream until someone calls the police.

In here, though? I'm in as much danger as I was down in that cellar.

"Let me just get dressed and grab my keys," Sean says.

He gives me a peck on the forehead and disappears back upstairs into his bedroom. I am tempted to run out the door right now, but then Sean emerges from the bedroom to shout something about taking vitamins when I'm sick and something about him never getting sick because of the supplements he takes.

I listen only vaguely. I'm just waiting in the middle of the living room with my hands folded, impatient to get out of here but focused on not being too obvious about it.

"Okay. Let's go," Sean comes downstairs fully dressed and with a coat on.

"Thanks, Sean." I smile at him.

We make it to the door, and then Sean starts patting his pockets.

"Now, where did I put those keys..." he says.

He turns around to look over my shoulder, checking every pocket. When he's done with that, he goes through them again, groaning loudly.

"It's fine. If you can't find them, I'll just get an Uber. I don't want to bother you with giving me a ride anyway."

"No, no. They're here somewhere, I just... Right." He raises a finger. "I just remembered. I left them upstairs in the bedroom. I'm really out of it today, forgetting things in places they're not supposed to be."

That final sentence sends a chill down my spine, but I offer him a vague smile at that. "Don't worry about it. I'll just get an Uber."

I pull my phone out. I hope my hands aren't trembling too much as I enter the application. I'm focused on the screen so much that the loud click at the door startles me. I look up to see Sean holding the lock of the door, a saddened look on his face.

"You know I can't let you go," he says.

Chapter 21

The cat's out of the bag. No more pretending, no more lying.

But I can't move. I feel as though sudden movement might make Sean lunge toward me.

I gulp, my throat dry as if I just swallowed a handful of sand. I can't find my tongue to speak.

"I'm sorry you had to find out like this," Sean says.

"Wh-what do you mean? F-find out what?" I ask.

He rolls his eyes. "Melissa, baby. Come on. You know I'm not stupid. And neither are you."

He steps toward me, and I backpedal instinctively.

"Don't be afraid of me," he says.

But I am. I am very afraid of him. I see in those eyes a deranged psychopath who's going to do anything in his power to keep me to himself like a prized possession.

I try to think of a way out of this situation. The phone is in my hand, and I could dial 911, but Sean would be on me before I even input the digits. The door is in front of me, but it's locked, and Sean is in the way. Even if I did manage to get out, I'd still need to get past the gate, and Sean has the remote for that attached to his keys.

I'm trapped, and Joshua won't be coming to my rescue this time.

So, I do the only thing that comes to my mind—I talk in hopes of buying myself some time.

"Anna called," I say.

The corner of his lip curves into a lopsided grin. He doesn't seem shocked, just amused.

"Why didn't you tell me?" I ask.

"Tell you what? That I'm the one with the mental condition, and not her?"

He takes a bigger step toward me. I back away once more, determined to keep my distance from him. I look left and right for anything I can use as a weapon. My eyes fall on my purse on the living room couch.

I look back at Sean and try to determine if I can reach it before him. I need to distract him to make it happen; otherwise, he'll beat me to it.

"Everything I did was because I love you, Melissa," he says. "I've always loved you, ever since the first day I laid my eyes on you."

"Yes. I know." I try to sound calm now. Strangely, it makes me feel like I'm in control at least a little bit. "I know. I saw the pictures."

That's when Sean's eyes go wide. He didn't know that I knew about it. He quickly tries to hide it by smiling.

"Tell me the truth, Sean. What happened that night when Joshua broke in?" I ask.

The only reason why I say Sean's name is because I want it to seem like I don't retain animosity toward him. In truth, just speaking it makes my mouth feel bitter.

Sean shakes his head. "Everything I did was to protect you. And I'll always do everything in my power to protect you because I love you more than anything."

My eyes drift to the purse on the couch again.

"Don't," Sean says.

But I don't listen. I break into a dash to the couch while Sean sprints after me. Just before I reach the purse, I feel strong arms tightening around my waste. My fingers hook the shoulder strap of the purse.

Sean is pulling me backward. I'm kicking with my feet, but they're uselessly dangling in the air. It doesn't matter. I'm already reaching into my purse for the pepper spray.

"Stop!" Sean shouts as he gropes to take the purse away from me.

The next thing I know, I'm flying sideways, and the floor is rushing to meet me. I instinctively put my hands out in front of myself to shield my face, but I drop the purse in the process. Pain explodes in my knee from the fall.

I plant my palms on the floor and push myself up. I twist my head to see Sean holding my purse with one hand and rummaging through it with the other. Moments later, he pulls out the pepper spray.

"This is what you've been looking for, right?"

He spins the object in his fingers teasingly then tosses it on the floor. The pepper spray rolls under the couch, devoured by the darkness. It's gone.

I scramble to my feet and run up the stairs. I expect to feel Sean's hand closing around my ankle at any moment and to be pulled back down the stairs, but by the time I'm at the top, I hear him shouting at me from downstairs.

"You can't run away from me, Melissa!"

I open the first door I come across and barge inside. It happens to be the bedroom. I slam the door behind me and lock it. I don't know how long the door will hold.

"I'm coming upstairs, Melissa!" I hear Sean's muffled voice.

Oh God. What do I do?

I don't have my phone on me. I dropped it when I ran to grab the purse. Now I'm without both—phone and pepper spray.

Frantically, I look around for a way out. I approach the window, open it, and peer below. A sense of vertigo overcomes me as I estimate whether I can safely land.

No way in hell.

It's way too high, and there's nothing but concrete to greet me below. In the best-case scenario, I'd break both my legs. Then I'd be utterly at Sean's mercy.

I hear footsteps climbing the stairs, slowly and menacingly. I imagine Sean deliberately stamping his feet on each step to announce his arrival. Why, though? To warn me? To scare me?

"Melissa," his voice comes from the other side of the door.

I hear the door handle jangling, and then there's a knock.

"Melissa, open this door," he says.

I stand perfectly still. After a moment of silence, he bangs on the door loudly enough for me to gasp in shock. I spin to look for another way out. I've effectively trapped myself in this room.

Just then, the entire door rattles violently. He's trying to break in. I do the only thing I can think of.

I crawl under the bed.

Stupid, I know, but panic does strange things to the brain.

Sean rams the door over and over. I hear wood splintering, and then the door bursts open and hits the opposite wall. I clamp hands over my mouth to stop myself from screaming. My heart is thudding against my chest so violently that I expect Sean to hear me right away.

I can see Sean's feet as he casually strolls inside the room and paces around the bed.

"Come on, Melissa. Just give me a chance to explain myself," he says. "I know this all seems bad, but just hear me out."

I don't fall for the trap. I remain quiet. He still hasn't looked under the bed, and I can't tell if he's toying with me or if he really doesn't know where I am.

"I knew you'd never agree to go out with me if you knew I'd been following you," he says. "You'd think I'm crazy. But look at us now. Look what we have built together. You fell in love with me in these past few weeks. That shows that we were meant to be together."

I want to shout at him that this is all sick and that the only reason I thought I loved him was because he manipulated me into believing he was a different kind of person. Beneath that veil of kindness, sweetness, and confidence was a sickness that was rooted too deeply in him.

He went out of his way to make it seem like our relationship was serendipity, but in reality, he was orchestrating everything to be exactly how he wanted it.

"I know you have a lot of questions," he says, still pacing slowly back and forth. "Those other girls... what I said about them was the truth. Ever since I fell in love with you, I started dating girls who look like you. I kept trying to find the perfect clone of you, but it was useless. I could find someone who looked like you, but once we started talking, I realized they were just a bad copy. I wanted the real thing. I wanted *you*."

He opens the closet, then slams it shut. "And then we matched on Tinder. Believe me, even that was difficult to pull off. But I knew we'd never be truly happy as long as Joshua was still in the picture."

I can't believe what I'm hearing. Is this really all true? Did he really plan all of this to such detail?

Sean walks up to the window, opens it, closes it, then says, "Do you know how much trouble it was to get rid of Joshua for you? I deliberately lured him here by sending him that text. I locked you in the cellar, and when he broke in, I allowed him to knock me out and "rescue" you. It was risky, but I knew you would see things how I wanted you to. Things could have gone wrong in so many ways that night, but they didn't, thanks to you."

He's sick. He's really, really sick. I had no idea how bad it was until I hear him saying all those things. I realize what a terrible mess I've gotten myself into. It could cost me my life. That understanding makes me want to crawl out from under the bed and run back down the stairs.

There's no way I can do that, of course. Sean will catch me long before I even get up onto my feet. So, I gulp against the panic swelling my chest and wait, praying that Sean will leave the room.

That doesn't happen, of course. He would have been too stupid not to check under the bed.

Before I know what's going on, Sean is peeking under the bed at me, a creepy grin on his face. I scream as he reaches for me and forcibly pulls me out. I thrash against him and caterwaul as he tries to speak, but I can't hear him over my own voice.

I think I catch my name and words like "calm down," but I can't calm down. Sean is holding me by the shoulders while I buck against him. Accidentally, I kick the nightstand, and it sends the expensive vase toppling to the floor—the same one I almost knocked down so many times in the past few weeks.

"Let me go, you freak!" I shout.

"Stop!" he shouts, but I don't listen,

Then, I hear a loud crack, and my ears are ringing. It takes me a moment to understand Sean has just slapped me. The shock and disorientation are enough to make me go quiet and limp.

That is a huge mistake because, by the time I realize what's going on, I feel Sean's fingers wrapping around my throat. I try to inhale, but my windpipe is being crushed so tightly that it's impossible to do so. I claw at his fingers, trying to pry them open, but they're gripping me like a vise.

"I didn't want to do this!" Sean says.

I see him above me, his face contorted in a grimace as he squeezes my neck. I don't want to die like this. I don't want his face to be the last thing I see before I leave this world.

"Why did you have to ruin what we have?!" he hisses. "We were so happy together!"

Stop. Please, just let me go, I think because I can't speak.

The corners of my vision grow dark. I realize in that moment that Sean doesn't care that he's going to kill me. He's off his medication, and he will become aware of what he's done only after I'm already dead. The opportunity I had to persuade him to let me go is now gone because I can't make a single sound.

"But you'll see things my way. I promise you," he says. "If you spend enough time with me, you'll see how much I love you. No one is ever going to love you as much as I do. I promise you."

It makes me think he plans on keeping me alive, but the crushing weight on my throat doesn't abate, which only confirms that he doesn't realize he's killing me.

My lungs are burning, desperate to get some air into them. My head feels like it's going to explode. If I don't do something in the next minute or so, I'm going to die.

I grope the floor for anything I could use as a weapon. I feel nothing, and then...

A round, hard outline comes in touch with my fingers. I vaguely realize it's the expensive vase. It fell, but it hasn't broken. I remember all the times I asked Sean to remove that vase because I had been so terrified of breaking it.

I'm glad he didn't listen.

I close my fingers around the rim and swing as hard as I can. I hear a loud shattering noise above me and Sean groaning. The pressure on my throat instantly releases, and a surge of air flows into my lungs.

I scramble to my feet, coughing, my hands holding my painful throat. Sean is holding a hand over the side of his face. Blood is trickling from his temple, the shards of the vase at his feet. Our eyes meet, and I know I won't get another chance.

I push myself onto my feet and run to the door.

"Melissa!" Sean shouts after me, and his voice is no longer riddled with concern.

It's full of unfiltered rage.

I race down the stairs, but I'm in such a hurry that I trip and tumble down the final few steps. Pain jolts my wrist, and I don't have time to think whether it's broken. I practically run into the front door, unlock it, swing it open and—

Before I can step outside, something crashes into me from behind, causing me to stumble forward.

"You're not going anywhere!" Sean shouts.

He's on top of me, and he's flipping me on my back. I dread feeling his fingers coiling around my neck again, but then I see him raising his hand with something sharp in it. It's a shard of the vase, I realize, and I can see that he's squeezing it so hard that it's drawing blood from his palm.

"You ungrateful bitch!" he shouts.

"Sean, wait! Please!" I raise my hands, but he doesn't look like he's about to relent.

"I love you!" I shout.

Sean freezes. His eyes widen. A dirty trick? Maybe, but my life is at stake. I don't care what I need to tell Sean to stay alive.

I see Sean's lips curving into a loving smile.

That moment of his hesitation is ultimately what saves my life.

I hear loud cracks, and Sean's body is jerking above me, red dots appearing on his chest. He looks down at the bullet holes then at me, a look of utter betrayal. Then, he falls sideways.

His eyes continue staring at me even when there's no life in them anymore, even when the police officers drag me away from the house.

Epilogue

How does a person even begin to recover after something like that?

When you're forced to do it, it's a lot easier than you'd think. I tell myself that things could have gone a lot worse. I could have died. Instead, I got off with only a broken wrist and a bruised throat.

I did not look forward to going through the entire ordeal with the detectives once again. Their investigation was a lot more thorough this time, and they managed to confirm that everything Sean had confessed to me was the truth.

Joshua had been innocent the entire time. He was still charged with breaking and entering, and he ended up having to pay a small fine. I haven't talked to him since. I can't.

Although I feel guilty that I rushed to blame him for locking me inside the cellar, I can't bring myself to see him in person and offer an apology. Too many things have happened between us, and I really don't want to reopen old wounds.

From what I understand, he's not too eager to talk to me, either. It's better that way. A part of me was afraid that Joshua would continue trying to contact me once he was no longer in custody. I'm not too happy about the fact that he hates me, but I don't blame him.

I almost ruined his life.

As for Rachel, she feels immensely guilty. She says that, if she never invited Sean over to force me into meeting with him, none of this would have happened.

That's not true, though. I already liked Sean and was just waiting for the right moment to reply to him. I just took my sweet time doing so.

In fact, I keep telling Rachel she saved my life by warning me about Sean lying about his work background and calling the police. She didn't even know if I was really in danger or not, but she called and lied anyway, just to get them to rush over to Sean's place.

I owe her my life because of it.

Months have passed, and on one snowy day, I exit Starbucks and hear someone call my name. I hate it when that happens in public. I always spin around, paranoid, looking for the person calling to me, expecting trouble.

The person who stands in front of me is tiny and has curly, brown hair.

"Uh, hi?" I say.

Is she even the one who called my name? The only indication that I have of that is the fact that she's making eye contact and smiling at me.

"I'm sorry, you don't recognize me. I'm Anna," she says.

My heart lurches into my throat.

"Oh," I say.

I don't know how she knows me, and I don't know why she wants to talk to me. You'd think that the person responsible for the death of your brother would be a lot more hostile if she ran into you, but Anna keeps that friendly smile on her face.

Maybe she's just like Sean. Maybe she's a manipulator waiting to get me away from other people so she can have her revenge on me.

"I'm sorry. I didn't mean to scare you," Anna says. "I hadn't ever planned on getting in touch with you, but then I saw you here... I recognized you from a picture Sean had sent me, you see."

"Okay." I nod.

I'm already halfway turned toward the exit, ready to end this interaction and be on my way. I can already tell I'm going to replay this encounter in my head throughout the entire day, and I hate it.

"Look, I don't want to bother you or anything like that, but can we talk?"

"I'm sorry. I'm really in a hurry right now," I say.

I turn to leave, but her hand gently finds my wrist.

"Just five minutes. Please," Anna says.

The look in her eye tells me there's no malicious intent there. She just wants closure.

"We can find a seat here, but I really have to go soon," I say.

"Thank you so much." Anna nods gratefully.

We find a nearby table to sit at. Anna crosses her fingers and stares at me. She's tapping her foot on the floor.

"So?" I ask.

I don't want to be rude because she's lost a brother. But I've been through hell myself, and I don't need to go through it again.

"First of all, allow me to say how very sorry I am for everything Sean did," Anna says.

I rotate the cup of coffee in my hands but say nothing.

"It's my fault it came to that. If I hadn't..." Anna looks down at her hands then back up at me. "I thought that if I allowed him to live a luxurious lifestyle in our parents' house, made him comfortable, that he would get better."

"Your parents' house?" I ask.

"Yes. That house belonged to our parents. They left it to us after they died, but since my work is out of town, I let Sean stay in it. I thought it would help give him a sense of normalcy."

"That explains why he was so rich. I can't believe I bought the whole story of him being a successful businessman."

Anna nods. "Sean didn't have a job. He couldn't hold onto a job for more than a few days. And it was evident that jobs only worsened his condition. After a while, I figured it was best if he stopped applying and focused on his mental health."

"But it didn't work."

"No. It only made him worse. It gave him time to feed his obsession."

"I don't understand. Why was he so fixated on me?"

Anna sighs. "You and Sean knew each other before you started dating."

"We did?"

I realize that I'm rotating the cup in my hand faster, so I leave it alone. I don't know if I want to know whatever Anna wants to tell me, but I'm in too deep to stop.

"Yes. You went to the same high school. But he got bullied until he dropped out and then later legally changed his name from Steve to Sean. I couldn't fathom why he would do that at the time."

"What?!" My eyes widen in disbelief. "Steve? Scrawny Steve?"

Anna smiles, but it's a somber one. "You were nice to him in his darkest time during high school. No one had ever been nice to him before that. He saw that as a sign that the two of you were meant to be together. That's why he asked you out that one time."

My mind is still processing the fact that Sean is actually Steve. He'd changed so much since high school. He became more muscular. The zits on his face were gone. He no longer stuttered...

But the crazed look was still there. I was just too blind to see it.

Anna continues talking. "He talked about you for years even after high school was over, you know. And then we warned him it was unhealthy, and the doctors warned him, too. He stopped talking about you, but I now know he never gave up his obsession."

"I know," I say. "I found his camera full of pictures of girls that looked like me."

"Yeah." Anna nods.

"Are they... I mean, did he...?" I can't bring myself to finish the question.

"They're okay," Anna says, and I breathe a sigh of relief. "The police were able to locate all of them. I spoke to a few of them. They found Sean via an ad he posted somewhere. Apparently, he was looking for girls who he could pay to pretend to be his girlfriends for the hour."

"I see," I say.

Those kinds of ads aren't unheard of. I've heard of people posting ads asking girls to pretend to be their moms and other kinds of weird things.

"But not just any kind of girlfriend," Anna says then hesitates.

"He wanted them to be me," I finish her sentence.

"Yes." Anna nods, embarrassed, "I spoke to one of them. She says the role play got too real for her. She kicked him in the groin and got out of there within twenty minutes."

"Why didn't any of them go to the police?"

"What for? Sean was acting weird, sure, but they had nothing to go to the police for. It's not like he held them captive there anyway."

"I see."

"Then he told me that he met a nice girl, and I thought he was really, finally getting better. Until he showed me your picture. That's when I knew he needed to be committed to a hospital."

I don't say anything to that. Anna and I both know how the rest of the event played out—Sean realized I knew too much. He tried to kill me, and the police shot him dead before he could harm me with a shard of the vase.

"I'm sorry," I say.

Anna looks surprised. "What are you sorry for? It's not your fault any of this happened."

"I know, but... I understand it's still hard to lose a family member."

"Yeah," Anna says. "But there's also strange comfort in there. I knew Sean was a threat to the world, but I was too blind to do anything about it. My love for him made me blind to his sickness. In a sense, I think this is the only good outcome. At least, he can't hurt anyone anymore."

There's a moment of silence between us if you're not counting the hubbub of people buzzing to and fro, grabbing their coffee. Finally, Anna forces a smile.

"Well, I've wasted enough of your time." She pushes her chair back and stands. "I guess I just wanted you to know the truth. I also wanted to see you, to see that you're okay, and to tell you how sorry I am for everything Sean did to you."

I continue to sit. I give her a weak nod and a ghost of a smile. I then call out to her.

"Anna?"

Anna starts to leave but then turns around to face me.

"Thank you for telling me the truth," I say.

She smiles. She turns to leave but then hesitates again. "I just want you to know one thing. Sean wasn't a bad person. He never meant to hurt anyone. He was just too sick."

"I understand," I say.

I don't want to say whether I agree or disagree with her because I'm not sure where I stand. Anna gives me one final smile, and then she's out of the shop.

For a moment, I stare at my coffee cup. I raise it to my lips and take a sip, thinking about the conversation with Anna.

I still haven't forgiven Sean for doing what he did. One day, I might, but not today. The trauma is still too fresh. I'll heal from it one day, and when I do, Sean's face will be nothing but a blur in a distant memory.

In the meantime, though, I think I'm going to take a break from dating. I deserve some me time.

And when I do get back into it again, I'll make sure to do a full background check of the guy I'm meeting.

THE END

Printed in Great Britain
by Amazon